A burst of noise surprised her...

The door opened and skiers chatting excitedly, entered the resort. Kyle's heart missed a beat as Fier approached her.

"I see you're here," said the man who had brought Kyle halfway across the world. "Have you seen your room? Do you have everything you need?"

"Yes." Kyle started nervously, but then something inside her snapped. No, dammit, she had *not* got everything she needed. She was entitled to some explanation, and she would demand it right now—before his two dark pools of eyes could drill a hole right through her.

"No," she said, "I haven't! I want to know what right you have to bring me here!"

He smiled, an alarming glint of white in his dark face. "None."

The Flight of the Golden Hawk

Sheila Strutt

Harlequin Books

TORONTO • NEW YORK • LOS ANGELES • LONDON
AMSTERDAM • PARIS • SYDNEY • HAMBURG
STOCKHOLM • ATHENS • TOKYO • MILAN

Original hardcover edition published in 1982
by Mills & Boon Limited

ISBN 0-373-02562-9

Harlequin Romance first edition July 1983

Printed in U.S.A.

CHAPTER ONE

'If all else fails, you'll just have to marry him, that's all!'

Kyle Haultain looked at her younger sister. She could never tell when Grace was joking, and it had seemed that way almost since she had been born. Even when Grace had been lying in the family heirloom cradle, turning the stream of people who had come to visit Thea and the unexpected new arrival into lifelong admirers, Grace had had that same expression of enigmatic amusement on her baby face.

It was probably wind, their father had explained to the five-year-old Kyle, hanging over the cradle with her long brown pigtails dangling. Grace couldn't even focus her absurdly large and dark blue eyes, far less be amused by what she saw. It was probably wind, Ash Haultain had explained, seizing the opportunity to take the baby from the cradle under the nose of a disapproving nanny and hold her lovingly against his shoulder.

But was it?—even at five Kyle had wondered as the big blue eyes had watched her unblinkingly over their father's shoulder; the baby head wobbly and covered with pale blonde fluff and so small and fragile compared to the handsome one beside it.

Was it wind, or was Grace not only quite aware but also inwardly amused by the power she seemed to exercise over everyone who came near her? At less than two weeks old, she had already left no room for another daughter in their father's love.

The twenty-two-year-old Grace now flicked her cigarette away with one hand and used the other to smooth a tendril of hair back from her smooth white forehead; no longer baby fluff but a thick, rich gold mane, cut to frame her perfect heart-shaped face.

'Don't look so stricken, Kylie,' she directed. 'We've still got several other options open to us before we need sacrifice your maidenhood!' She grinned. Grace's 'saving grace'—her grin. Impish and engaging, it turned her from a spoiled young beauty, well aware of her power to charm and turn every other woman in a room into second best, into . . . well, Grace!

She began to tick the options off on long, slender fingers while Kyle made a mental note to pick up the still burning cigarette. Manuel would not approve of the billiard table surface of his lawn being used as an ashtray, even though his imperfect English and innate good manners would probably prevent him saying it. And Manuel also adored Grace.

'Our first hope is that our revered cousin will choose to leave well alone and let us go on living here!' she said.

'But what would we live on?' Kyle asked doubtfully.

'Oh, don't be such a wet blanket! Something'll turn up!' Grace was not interested in minor points and, if you were Grace, something always did turn up. 'Perhaps you could get a proper job as a secretary,' she suggested.

'Perhaps.' A secretary's salary was hardly likely to keep a perfect example of a Georgian country home in the English countryside, to say nothing of the grounds and staff needed to run it, and even if Fier Cailloux was prepared to let them go on living there, he could hardly be expected to pay all their expenses. But, again, Grace would not be interested in the drawbacks, and Kyle kept her doubts to herself.

'Or maybe he'll decide to give it to the National Trust with some sort of clause written in that anyone living here at the time stays on rent free . . . that sort of thing.' Grace's clear white forehead wrinkled. 'Not that I'm all that keen on being a relic of the National Trust, but Dovercourt should be worth something to them, shouldn't it? Prinny slept here, or something, didn't he? That should be worth at least fifty pence a head to the paying customers! You could show them round—you've always been keen on history and that sort of thing.' She did a fair imitation of Kyle's much quieter voice. '. . . and in this bed, His Royal Highness, George, Prince of Wales, finally asked Mrs Fitzherbert to be his wife . . .! Or,' she dropped her tour guide voice, 'was it Mrs Fitzherbert who did the asking?'

Her laughter made Kyle suddenly annoyed. 'Grace, for heaven's sake, be serious!'

'I am serious, can't you see that?' Grace said sharply. 'I'm trying to get round the thought of exactly what's going to happen if the last of our ancient family decides he wants to live in the ancestral home and throws us out! With the best will in the world, I can hardly see him wanting two penniless female relatives to support.'

'Then you think he might?'

'What? Throw us out? Or decide to live here?' Grace's brow once more furrowed. 'In my more hopeful moments, I try and tell myself that he won't—want to live here, I mean. After all, what could an elderly Canadian possibly find to amuse him in a couple of hundred acres of Sussex countryside? He'll know no one; he'll be totally out of place, and it would probably drive him mad.'

'But what if he does want to?' Kyle persisted.

'I've told you!' Grace looked at her. 'That, my dear elder sister, is where you come in. You marry him!'

'Grace, don't be so ridiculous!' But even so, Kyle blushed.

'What's so ridiculous? You're twenty-seven. . . .' Twenty-eight, Kyle thought, but Grace had been abroad for most of the past year and, besides, she had never been too interested in family birthdays. 'And you're attractive,' Grace went on. 'Or at least you could be if you got rid of that hank of hair you like to hide behind and spent some money on a facial and new clothes.'

Money went on servants' wages, not new clothes. 'Thanks!' Kyle said wryly, but Grace didn't hear. Caught up in her new fantasy, she went rattling on. 'Fier Cailloux—the name's not bad, at least! Mrs Fier Cailloux——' she stretched and pursed her delicately tinted lips to exaggerate every syllable. 'Fee-air Kye-oo! Fier means proud, doesn't it?' she added on a sudden thought. 'Hardly the first name to spring to mind for a shopkeeper, or whatever it is he does, but then a shopkeeper's hardly the first sort of person to spring to mind when it comes to inheriting all this.' Her languid wave encompassed the house, the lawn and the huge old mulberry tree under which they were sitting, lingering, after tea. 'But the name's not bad— not bad at all!' She turned on Kyle with her impish grin. 'How does going through life as Mrs Fier Cailloux strike you?'

'I told you, you're being ridiculous!' Kyle got abruptly up from the white cane lawn chair and started to pile the used tea things on the tray. Manuel and Fernanda had enough to do just keeping up with the work in the house and grounds. They were not there to wait on them.

'Oh, for goodness' sake!' Grace made no attempt to help her. 'Stop behaving as if I'm planning on selling you into white slavery! It mightn't be so bad. After all, when this was built,' she nodded towards the dazzling façade of the house, 'arranged marriages were quite the thing. Love was a luxury if you wanted to stay rich.'

Tea on the lawn under an ancient mulberry tree; a view over the rolling Sussex countryside which, in spite of the property that had already had to be sold off, still did not extend beyond land owned by the estate and two sisters, as unalike as chalk and cheese but the last in the direct line of an ancient family, worrying about how to make ends meet.

Kyle at least agreed with Grace in one thing. Appearances could often be deceptive. But what Grace was suggesting as a solution to their problems was, like most of her ideas, outrageous.

'What's wrong,' she now asked sharply, 'about marrying for money?'

Kyle straightened from the tea tray. 'You're serious, aren't you?'

'Unless you can think of anything better, of course I'm serious!' Grace retorted. 'I'm certainly not going to let some Canadian hayseed get away with everything that should be ours, if that's what you think! I'd marry him myself if I wasn't tied to that fool Alexei for at least another two years.'

'But you don't even know what he's like!'

'I know enough!' the Countess Grace Orsinski said

imperturbably. 'Or at least, I know enough to make an educated guess.' She went back to ticking off points on her beautifully manicured fingers. 'One—he's unmarried. Two—he's old enough to be our father and three—he's only distantly related. *Very* distantly related,' she emphasised. 'And now he's also very rich. Oh, it's so unfair!'

She flung herself back on the padded cane chaise-longue in one long, fluid movement and glowered at the view. Even angry, Grace couldn't do an ungraceful thing.

'You've forgotten one thing,' Kyle couldn't resist teasing.

'Oh, what?' Grace enquired sulkily.

'As of now, he's also engaged to be married!'

'And why not?' Grace stopped glowering and gave her elder sister a sharp and quite dispassionate look. 'If you marry him, he's middle-aged already and he'll die first. You'll be legally entitled to inherit *something*, and even if it's only half and we split that half, that's still twenty-five per cent each. It's not much when we should get everything, but it's better than nothing at all. Oh, it's so unfair!' she repeated moodily. 'Why should some Canadian shopkeeper get all this just because he happens to be a man?'

'He also happens to be a Haultain,' Kyle pointed out.

'Yes, but only because his mother was,' Grace sulked. 'What did the solicitor's letter say? That he's part French, part Cree and part Iroquois: he's just one fourth part Haultain—just one fourth part—and it nets him everything! It's so unfair!' Her every speech for days had been dotted with the phrase. 'This is supposed to be the age of women's liberation, but we lose everything just because we didn't happen to be born men. Damn entailments! Damn ancestors who took it for granted that there'd always be sons to inherit so they made sure the daughters couldn't, and damn all Canadian shopkeepers!' she finished explosively.

'I can't understand why you're so sure he's a shopkeeper.' She would have to go and change soon, Kyle realised. It would hardly do to have her first meeting with Fier Cailloux—fourth part Haultain and a shopkeeper or not, wearing old shorts and a cotton top.

'What else can he be?' Grace said. 'The solicitor's letter said he was an outfitter. He's probably got one of those dreary little gents' clothing stores Alex and I saw when we went through Canada on our honeymoon. You can't imagine what they're like. Stuck away in one-horse towns with everything in acrylic or polyester and cans of kerosene and chicken feed stacked away out back in case they get snowed in!'

To Kyle it sounded rather nice—cosy and oldfashioned—but Grace had obviously not been impressed.

'And we do know he comes from a small town,' Grace pointed out. 'Faucon d'Or—what sort of name is that? A small town in the Rocky Mountains and too small to be on the map!'

They had spent hours poring over an old atlas after the solicitor's letter had arrived telling them that the last male heir of the Haultain line had finally been run to earth, but, even with the help of a magnifying glass, they had not been able to find the name Faucon d'Or. Hawk of gold: Kyle also thought that sounded rather nice.

'No,' Grace said finally, 'you mark my words. He'll turn out to be a hick from the back of nowhere with a forty-nine-inch waistline and a drooping grey moustache. He'll probably also go round calling us Ma'am. That's what Canadians do.' She grinned at the recollection. Another one of Grace's 'saving graces'—her bad moods rarely lasted long.

Kyle bent and picked up the tea tray. 'Well, we'll know soon enough. The London train gets in in forty minutes and it'll take him ten minutes from the station in the taxi. In less than an hour, we'll have seen all there is to see about him so, I'd better take this in and go and change.'

'Okay!' Grace reached into her slim gold case for another cigarette. 'You change—I'm not going to bother.'

She had no need to bother, Kyle thought as she took the loaded tray indoors. The cotton dress that looked so simple was, in fact, designer-made, and Grace could anyway wear a sack and get away with it. Not that the Countess Grace Orsinski would be reduced to wearing sacks just yet. When she had finally walked out on Alex, she had not forgotten to take her large and expensive wardrobe with her.

The kitchen was empty and cool after the sun outside. Manuel and Fernanda must be in their flat upstairs, and Kyle wondered if Fier Cailloux would want to keep the Spanish couple on as she began to wash the dishes. They had been lucky enough to get servants at all for a household which had no money for separate cars and colour televisions, and there wasn't even an important name—just an ancient one.

The first Haultain had raised his standard for William the Conqueror and had been rewarded with a fiefdom in this part of Sussex. Manor houses had been burned down or rebuilt until they had arrived at this present example of pure Georgian architecture, but there had been Haultains living at Dovercourt ever since. And now the name was gone—or almost. Grace had stopped being a Haultain when she was sixteen. First she was Hagib and now she was Orsinski, and when she got the divorce she had set her heart on, she would probably soon be something else. Grace was much too striking to remain alone for long.

Kyle finished the dishes and walked along a dark, narrow corridor to the green baize door that marked the dividing line between the servants quarters and the rest of a house that had been built in the full flowering of the Regency.

Had it always looked so shabby? Had the gilding on the elaborate plaster bosses on the hall ceiling always been so faded and the dust on the hanging crystal chandelier so obvious. Or was it because she was suddenly seeing everything through the eyes of the stranger who would soon be arriving? Kyle didn't know as she climbed the curving staircase. What she did know was that the Haultain who had built this house had built it in the expectation of a never-ending line of sons to succeed him, and now she was the last Haultain left. Even Fier Cailloux didn't have the name unless he assumed it.

Would he want to take the name, she wondered as she walked along the corridor to her room and began to change from shorts and top into a dress. The name couldn't bring the money necessary to run a house of this size and scale nowadays. They wouldn't have survived until now if Thea hadn't helped them out, and Thea certainly wouldn't be prepared to go on subsidising Dovercourt for the benefit of an unknown relative of the husband she had despised.

Thea! Kyle smiled. Thea had given her the dress she was now wearing. 'Serviceable', she had called it. A good match for the personality of the person wearing it, Kyle thought privately. She considered the brown shoulder-length hair that Grace had so disparagingly referred to as a 'hank' in the damp-stained mirror. It wasn't thick but fine and straight with a tendency to flop across her face. Useful, sometimes, when she wanted to hide herself, but today? She reached for a handful of pins and put them in her mouth. Today she would do better to put it up into a neat French pleat.

She worked quickly and efficiently, her sherry brown eyes steady with concentration above the hairpins in the compressed line of her mouth.

Fier Cailloux was almost bound to want to sell, but that would affect Grace more than it would affect her. She, as Grace had so rightly pointed out, could always get a job as a secretary. She had managed the estate ever since she had been old enough to be taken seriously, so she could certainly get a job, and as for her feelings about having to leave the only home she had ever known, she would keep them firmly under wraps and deal with them later on.

Meanwhile—she turned sideways on to the cloudy, floor-length mirror in its fruitwood stand and studied the slim young woman reflected there. Her hair was neat, her 'serviceable' linen dress, discreetly calf-length, hid what she knew were her best feature and what Grace quite openly referred to as her 'showgirl' legs, and she had ten minutes to go and set out the sherry ready for the arrival of the man who held both their futures in his hands. It was really quite remarkable how calm she could still be if she didn't let herself think ahead of those ten minutes.

The library overlooked the front of the house with another mulberry tree on the centre of the lawn going down to wrought iron gates, and she heard the sound of the engine coming up the drive just as she was setting the decanter on its silver tray. Her stomach turned over. The London train must have been early. Taking a deep breath, she went across to the window and looked out.

But it certainly wasn't the station taxi pulled up beside the shallow flight of steps leading up under the pillared portico. Kyle frowned in irritation. How could Grace be so inconsiderate! With Fier Cailloux arriving in ten minutes, she must have invited one of her legion of admirers to come for drinks, or else it was Alex, come on one of his sporadic attempts to persuade her to go back to him. They were like children, unable to live together or apart, but another stormy scene with Alex was the last thing she needed with Fier Cailloux, by now, already on his way. But the sleek cream sports car with the distinctive Mercedes symbol on its hood didn't belong to Alex, and Kyle stepped quickly back. Grace, presumably, was still in the garden and both back and front doors were wide open. If the driver of the car didn't see her standing there, he might go straight through the house in search of Grace.

'This is Dovercourt, isn't it?' It was less of a question than a statement.

'Yes.' There had been no sound of footsteps, but someone—a man—was definitely standing in the library doorway and if there was any diffidence, it was on her side. He stood there as if he owned it, balanced lightly on the balls of his feet with an expensive, dark blue pin-striped suit doing its best but failing to hide the outline of hard muscle underneath. A white silk shirt threw the deep tan of his face into dark relief and his hair was thick and black with one unruly lock falling across his forehead which he brushed impatiently back as she stood there, at a loss for words.

'Yes . . . yes, it is!' She finally finished what she had begun to say when she had spun round and found him standing there. She wondered why she was so suddenly apprehensive. This, obviously, was another one of Grace's suitors. Not her usual style; Grace liked to be indulged, not mastered, and this man was not the readily indulgent type. She didn't know how she knew it, but she did as annoyance began to overtake her slight tremor of apprehension. How could Grace be so inconsiderate? She hadn't even said she had invited anyone, and Fier Cailloux's taxi must be due to arrive at any minute from the station. 'Can I help you?' she said shortly.

He walked into the library and stood there looking round. It was a large room, but it suddenly seemed much smaller. 'Yes.' When he finally looked at her it was with eyes of a brilliant, unexpected cobalt blue. 'I'm here to see Miss Haultain. I'm expected. . . .'

'I'll go and get Grace.' Kyle was already starting towards the door when his next words rooted her to the spot.

'. . . tell her it's Fier Cailloux.'

The room went dead and it was a second before her ears came out of their long pressure dive and the ordinary, everyday sounds came crowding in. She must be wrong. This couldn't be Fier Cailloux. She was waiting for Grace's elderly bachelor with the drooping grey moustache. The real Fier Cailloux was still in the taxi driving from the station. She couldn't have heard what she thought she had. She must be wrong. She had to be!

'I'm sorry, I . . .' in spite of all her certainty, she stumbled, 'I'm afraid I didn't catch the name.'

'Fier Cailloux.' She hadn't been mistaken and impatience touched the eyes that watched her. 'I have an appointment with Miss Haultain.'

'Yes, I know.' What should she do now? Should she shake his hand? On balance, Kyle decided not. Instead, she stood there while all the careful words and phrases she had rehearsed vanished from her head.

'Then do you think you could go and tell her I've arrived?' he enquired eventually.

She heard the accent now; transatlantic touched with French and a hint of edge.

'I don't have to.' A pair of black eyebrows rose. 'Oh, I'm sorry!' Why was she behaving like a fool? Of course he wouldn't know. 'I'm Kyle Haultain.'

'You?' He made no effort to hide his incredulity. 'I assumed you were the housekeeper!' Another man might have apologised; he didn't, and Kyle had a fleeting vision of herself through his eyes—diffident, self-effacing, the perfect housekeeper in the pale grey linen dress. She, of all people, should understand his assumption. 'Weren't you told that I was coming?' He confirmed her thoughts. It was her mistake, not his.

'Yes . . . yes, of course. It was just that I was expecting someone different.' Kyle mentally kicked herself. It might be the truth but she had no need to say it.

'Really?' For the first time he looked amused and the blue eyes danced. 'And exactly what did you expect?' he enquired quietly.

Anything except a man of thirty-five or six with a

lock of jet black hair once more falling across his forehead to soften the severity of his face but not the sheer
force and magnetism stamping every inch of him. She
had noticed before and she noticed again how the ex-
pensively cut dark suit fought a losing battle to disguise
the muscle underneath into elegant conformity. He
indeed had elegance, but he had power, and the lines
that made his lean dark face his own and not that of a
conventionally handsome man told her that he also had
authority.

His mouth was firm and straight—too straight
except when he smiled with an alarming flash of strong
white teeth—his nose had a proud, high bridge and his
jaw was hard and strong. It was a dark face—naturally
dark, not just tanned as she had first thought—and it
was capable of holding secrets while the scrutiny of
brilliant cobalt eyes probed the thoughts of anyone
foolish enough to try and deceive him.

When the news had reached them that the heir to
Dovercourt had at last been found, it had been Grace
who had done the checking. Kyle had just accepted
that another phase in Dovercourt's long history was
coming to an end, but the elderly Canadian bachelor
Grace had predicted vanished into the realms of fairytale obscurity as she stood feet away from the real Fier
Cailloux and tried to answer him.

'We expected you to come by train from London,'
she said evasively. 'We didn't think you'd be here so
soon.'

'I drove—I hired a car.' He inclined his head in the
direction of the cream Mercedes parked on the
gravelled drive, but the brilliant cobalt eyes didn't
move an inch.

And he had probably driven at speeds well above

the limit, Kyle thought privately. 'Would you like some sherry?' she gestured towards the decanter on its tray.

'No.' Why wouldn't he stop watching her? 'I'd rather know your plans. You have a sister, don't you?'

'Yes—Grace.' Where *was* Grace? She would know how to deal with this situation; Grace had been winding men around her little finger all her life. The thought that this man wouldn't be so malleable once more flashed across Kyle's mind. 'I think she's in the garden—I'll go and get her.'

'No!' The word blocked her escape. 'You're the older sister, aren't you?'

'Yes.' He had also done his checking, Kyle acknowledged grudgingly. For most people, Grace was the *only* Haultain sister.

'Then I think you're entitled to hear what I have to say first. I've got a buyer for Dovercourt.' Kyle's heart sank. 'An American publisher with an English wife,' he went on bluntly, 'but I've not decided yet. A lot will depend on whether I can combine my business interests in Canada with what also has to be done here.'

The small town store Grace had dreamed up for him also faded into obscurity. Whatever Fier Cailloux did to make the money for the expensive clothes and the general aura of wealth that surrounded him, it wasn't running a single clothing store. Perhaps a chain; more probably an empire, Kyle decided, looking at the determined face.

'I know there are two farms and I'll visit them tomorrow,' he said flatly. 'Meanwhile, perhaps you can show me round the house.'

'Now?' Kyle was surprised.

'Why not?' He regarded her expressionlessly. 'I'm

here on a three-day business trip, not a holiday. I don't have time to waste.'

Kyle's practice as the tour guide Grace had suggested she become started as he stood back to allow her to precede him from the library and down the passageway to the green baize door leading to the servants' quarters.

Manuel and Fernanda had reappeared in the kitchen and Manuel, always small, now seemed tiny. Yet it wasn't entirely Fier's height and build—well over six feet and well proportioned—that put him head and shoulders above the Spanish houseman. It was the indefinable quality he carried with him, a quality that would make him stand out in any other room with any other man. Ancient, autocratic, powerful—Kyle struggled to find the right word. Although he was more European than Indian, it was Pound Maker she was seeing as he stood there, or any other one of the great North American Indian tribal chiefs. Except, of course, for those extraordinary cobalt eyes.

The extraordinary cobalt eyes were now fixed on Manuel. 'You're Manuel Seguera,' the owner of those eyes said firmly.

'Yes, sir.' Thumbs straight along the sides of his butler's apron, Manuel stood rigidly to attention. He was in England for the sole purpose of learning English. He never spoke anything else, but his grounding had come from English B-movies shown on Spanish television without the benefit of subtitles. Kyle sometimes wondered if they ever showed anything but war films, because his speech and deportment was that of a tiny, perfect sergeant-major in the British army.

His wife, Fernanda, was the one who struggled with

the aspirates and gutturals of a heavy Spanish accent. Manuel was determined to be letter perfect against the day when he finally achieved his dreams of owning his own holiday hotel on the Costa Brava.

Manuel Seguera! Kyle registered. Fier had certainly done his homework if he even knew the names of the staff at Dovercourt.

'Yes, sir,' Manuel repeated. 'This my wife, Fernanda.'

'*Señor!*' An entranced Fernanda almost dropped a curtsey.

'What do they do, this Spanish couple of yours?' They had moved on to the ornate dining room when Fier asked the question.

'Do?' Kyle was surprised he had to ask. 'Well, they clean, of course, and Manuel sees to the grounds.'

'Really?' He gave a narrow smile and Kyle was once more seeing the dust and general air of shabbiness through a stranger's eyes. Prinny had once dined in that dining room, but the splendour had long since disappeared and, like the whole house, it needed money and more money to be poured into it. Could she really blame Fier if he made up his mind to sell?—but now she was more concerned with Manuel and Fernanda.

'They do their best,' she said defensively, 'and I help. But it's a big house. My mother pays their wages. . . .'

'That's Thea Robertson.' Fier paused in his inspection of the portraits that lined the walls. Another instance of his checking! How many people knew that Thea Robertson had been married to Ash Haultain? Once, when the publicity value of the love story of a minor actress and the head of one of England's oldest families had been worth noticing, both the tabloids and the glossies had been full of stories and photographs about the unlikely marriage, but Ash Haultain and Thea Robertson as a couple had long ago lost public interest.

Thea, it was true, had gone on to become a news item in her own right. Enormously beautiful and hardly less talented, she was still a force, not only in the world of the theatre but in the gossip columns, with her succession of barely disguised young lovers.

Ash Haultain, though, had dropped out of sight. An introspective archaeologist, he had lost the battle with his wife's career soon after Grace had been born—perhaps before—and he had gone off to Kenya to pursue his investigations into the mystery of man's origins.

The last time Kyle had seen her father, she had been twenty-one. He had come back to Dovercourt for a month and, at the end of that month, he had left and taken the fifteen—almost sixteen—year-old Grace with him. It was almost as if he had known that an end had come to the long series of servants and governesses who had taken care of them, and he had taken the daughter he loved best. Grace had married her first husband six months later.

Did Fier also know, Kyle wondered, that her father's part in her life had been so shadowy that, when he died, it had been like hearing of the death of a virtual stranger? Did that account for his heir's lack of sympathy for Ash Haultain's recent death?

There was no way of telling from the impassive face now watching her against a background of the Haultain family portraits.

'Have we seen everything downstairs?' he asked.

'Yes.'

'Okay, then, we'll go upstairs.' He took it for granted she would follow, and, studying the set of the shoulders that moved ahead of her, Kyle had an irrational feeling of security. Fier Cailloux might be many things, but he would never be shadowy. She found herself wondering if Grace's assumption that he was unmarried was also untrue, and she pushed the thought aside. That was none of her concern, and, if she had needed proof, the man whose broad-shouldered, slim-hipped back she was now following had more than given it. She could still remember the scepticism in the unusually accented voice when he discovered she was not the housekeeper. It wasn't the first time Kyle had found herself wishing that it was she, not Grace, who had inherited the Thea Robertson attraction. But it was Grace who had their mother's blondeness and personality. She was her father's daughter, with her brown hair and eyes and much quieter nature. Grace's suggestion for saving Dovercourt was quite ridiculous. No one—and certainly not a man like Fier Cailloux— would even consider marrying her.

'That's my room.' She said it as Fier paused with his hand on the half open door. The bed, the mirror, the faded curtains; they all looked so shabby. Had they always looked like that, or was it that she was just used to it?

'I see.' He closed the door without a further comment. 'And this one?' He walked on to the next room.

'That belongs to Grace—my sister,' she added as he looked puzzled.

This must be a first. No one ever forgot Grace. But then Fier hadn't met her, Kyle remembered. He hadn't been exposed to the gold and white fairytale princess beauty that left men at first incredulous and then her slaves for life. It was fortunate, though, that Grace wasn't there to hear him. Whether they had met or not, Fier must know of her spectacular attraction—he certainly knew of everything else—and Grace would not have been impressed by his momentary lapse.

'Is she in there?'

'No. She's downstairs in the garden. But I'm sure she wouldn't mind if we went in.'

Taking her explanation as permission, Fier opened the door and Kyle saw that she had been wrong. Grace was not only there, she was reflected in the mirror, so that there were two Graces who turned to greet him in a floating haze of pale sea green. One the Grace of flesh and blood in the Valentino sea green sheath with floating panels which had replaced the earlier, simpler, cotton dress, and the other a reflection of her naked back and glorious mane of hair, silvered by the sunlight bouncing off the oval floor-length mirror. For his first sight of her, Fier saw the whole and total Grace. No wonder he stopped short, and no wonder Kyle heard his sharp intake of breath. For the first time since he had arrived at Dovercourt, Fier Cailloux had been taken by surprise.

He finally moved forward and his face appeared beside Grace in the mirror, wearing that same half stunned expression that Kyle had seen on the faces of so many men before when they caught their first sight of Grace. The only difference was that, this time, it was the strongest face she had ever known that was softening through all the usual stages of reaction to an awestruck admiration for Grace's pale gold beauty.

It had taken just a second, but it seemed much longer before she heard her own quiet voice. 'This is my sister Grace. Grace—this is Fier Cailloux.'

CHAPTER TWO

FERNANDA had produced Chateaubriand for dinner. At least, Kyle had cooked it and Fernanda had arranged it in the silver serving dish surrounded by its garnish of tiny new potatoes and a bouquet of fresh vegetables from Manuel's kitchen garden. Manuel himself had served, delighted to have a meal which at last tested his skill as an expert butler.

For one short evening, the faded dining room seemed to have recovered all its former glory with Fier sitting at the head of the long table, elegant in dinner jacket and ruffled shirt, and Grace—automatically on his right—and Kyle on either side of him. Candles flickered on the table and a bowl of Dovercourt nectarines and peaches stood in the centre, but, for all the trouble and expense, Kyle realised, she might just have well served one of the more usual Dovercourt evening meals to be eaten in the smaller breakfast room.

Fier ate and drank, but all the time, his eyes were fixed on Grace.

'Have you ever been to Cannes?' As always, Grace was blooming under the interest of a new and attractive—an unusually attractive—man.

'No, I haven't. Why?' Fier's eyes held a soft gleam.

'Because you should.' Grace paused; outrageous and provocative as she tilted her head and lowered her eyes demurely above the daringly low neckline of her dress. 'Cannes is full of beautiful men, but it could always use one more!' Her lips curved and she looked up,

25

giving him the full dramatic benefit of huge violet eyes
in a setting of long dark lashes. 'Perhaps I should take
you there and show you round myself!'

'Grace . . .!' Kyle's scandalised protest was lost in
Fier's quiet chuckle.

'An intriguing prospect, but not possible. I'm
afraid,' he said. 'In three days I shall be back in
Canada.'

It must be the candlelight that made his face expressionless. Kyle knew that if she could see it clearly, it
must hold that same mixture of longing and regret that
she had seen on so many masculine faces when their
owners were denied time alone in Grace's company.
Except that it was usually they who had given the invitation and been refused, not the other way around.

The light was certainly clear enough to see the way
Fier watched her as Grace went chattering on. He
couldn't take his eyes from her.

'But you can't be going back to Canada so soon!'
Grace's surprise caught her ear and Kyle began to
listen. This was a conversation that touched them both.
Apart from his mention of a prospective buyer, Fier
had given no firm indication of his plans either for
himself or, far more importantly, for Dovercourt.

'But I am. On Thursday.' He reached for his glass
with long brown fingers.

'I see.' Grace stopped. She must also have been
affected by a sixth sense that this was not a man to be
questioned closely, Kyle realised.

'I have to get back to Faucon d'Or,' Fier explained.
'A ranch won't run itself.'

'A ranch?' Grace's surprise was obvious. 'But we
thought you were a . . .' Her voice tailed off.

'A storekeeper!' Kyle could remember her disgust.

'A storekeeper—a common shopkeeper and he gets all this!' There was no doubt that Grace had changed her atittude towards storekeepers in the past two hours, but Kyle could still remember her clear-voiced contempt as she had sat on the lawn behind Dovercourt and faced the fact that everything she could see had already passed into the hands of someone who was so obviously socially inferior.

'You thought what?' The dawning gleam in Fier's dark eyes spread to become an alarming flash of white in his tanned face.

For once Grace was discomfited and she looked from his smile to the half-eaten nectarine on her plate. 'We thought you owned a store,' she muttered.

This time he laughed, and Kyle saw her sister flush. No one ever laughed at Grace.

'Well, what else were we to think?' she asked petulantly. 'We were told you were an outfitter!'

'An outfitter, my dear young lady, doesn't run a store!' He took pity on her. Another first for Grace; no one ever pitied Grace. Or condescended to her. 'The original outfitters supplied the old Hudson Bay forts and then they took supplies through to the miners. Some of them led the wagon trains out to California— they helped build the West from the Rockies down to Mexico. They went over country no white man had ever seen before and they were hard men and tough. Some of them were part Indian——' One part Iroquois and one part Cree: the information the solicitor had given them started to make sense as Fier for ever put to rest their preconceived image of the new owner of Dovercourt as a middle-aged small-town shopkeeper.

Kyle could see him in the mountains. In spite of the

immaculate evening clothes, the man who wore them could belong nowhere else.

'Around the turn of the century the tourists started to come out West and my grandfather——' he paused, choosing his words carefully, '——*acquired* a hunting lodge. I run it now, in the last of the wilderness.' For an instant he was back there; not the French or English part of him but all Indian as he saw the limitless horizons and the solitude.

'Then you must have heard of Alex!' In the library much later, Grace was once more confident.

'Alex?' Fier looked questioning.

'Count Alexei Orsinski,' Grace explained. 'My husband.'

With his back to the empty fireplace, Fier shot her a long hard look over the glass of brandy in his hand. 'I didn't know you were married.'

'I was.' Husbands were no more than a fitting tribute, Grace implied. 'We're separated now——' was it Kyle's imagination or did the tension in Fier's strongly muscled legs relax? It was hardly surprising if it had. To meet the most beautiful woman you had met in a long time and then discover she was, apparently, married would be a shock for any man. '——Alex adores shooting things,' Grace was going on. 'It comes of having been brought up in France—all those heads and horns and things! Ugh!' She gave a charming little shudder.

Fier sipped his brandy. 'We don't hunt game at Faucon d'Or,' he said mildly. 'We preserve, observe and enjoy.'

What he said was not what Kyle expected, but Grace smiled.

'Then you're exactly like Alexei,' she said brightly: the point had missed her. 'He loves looking at his trophies. We've got this villa near Cannes——' a curious slip, Kyle thought. Grace was always saying that if she never saw Alex Orsinski again it would be too soon, and yet she was still referring to his home as theirs, '—and he has a room absolutely plastered with stuffed animals. Ugh!' She repeated the charming little shudder. 'It's all too gruesome! Let's change the subject. Would you like another drink?'

She went across to take his brandy glass, her hand brushing against his.

'No—no, thanks.' Fier put the glass on the marble overmantel behind him and there was a long, long pause.

'Then you won't be keeping Dovercourt, I suppose?' Grace said it, but Kyle froze in her seat behind the coffee tray.

'Really?' He looked quizzical. 'And why do you suppose that?'

'Oh, I don't know. . . .' Grace stopped, waiting for him to come to her assistance, but then she shrugged. 'Well, if you've got a ranch and now that you've seen how run-down this place is, it's hardly likely, is it?' She gave a brittle laugh. 'I've told Kyle she ought to make you marry her, then we can go on living here!'

'You've what?' The dark eyes suddenly switched to Kyle as if seeing her for the first time.

'Grace . . .!' Kyle wished the floor would open up and swallow her.

'Well, it's obvious, isn't it?' Grace drifted towards the drinks table in a filmy haze of sea green gauze and lifted the decanter. It was her second brandy on top of wine at dinner, but even alcohol couldn't make her less than graceful. Just indiscreet and—Kyle writhed—totally embarrassing. She longed for Fier to look away, but he kept on watching her. A shiver started underneath her skin.

'You're a bachelor. At least,' Grace paused with the decanter and gave Fier a sharp look, 'I assume you are?'

'Yes.' The eyes let Kyle slip back into obscurity as they fastened back on Grace.

'Then it's simple, isn't it?' Grace continued with her foolhardy game. 'You marry Kyle and she can go on running Dovercourt and you can go on running . . .' she stumbled over the unfamiliar name, '. . . you can go on running Faucon d'Or.'

'And that's important to you?' he asked quietly.

'Of course!' Grace was reckless. 'Dovercourt's our home!'

'In that case,' Fier's eyes turned back to Kyle and the shiver started up again, 'I'll have to consider it.'

She had never driven in such an expensive car before. With the canvas roof of the Mercedes down and the wind tugging at her hair, Kyle sat back in the body-contoured leather seat and watched the hedges flashing by from her unaccustomed vantage point. Always, when they visited either of the farms that belonged to the estate, she was driving the old estate Land Rover and sitting on a level with the hedgerows. Now, lower down and sitting back, the hedgerows were no more than a blurred background to the alarming presence of the clear-cut profile just inches away from her.

It was sheer chance she was with Fier. Grace, who never went near either of the tenant farms, had pleaded a headache at the last moment. The thought had crossed Kyle's mind that it was a game, designed to have Fier persuade her and prove the hold she always had on men, but Fier had just regarded her across the breakfast table and, with a few words of formal sympathy, had accepted her suggestion that Kyle show him round the two farms in her place.

The morning had gone well. Surely—surely, now that Fier had met the Sullys and the Gibsons whose families had also been a part of Dovercourt for generations; now that they were no longer figures on a balance sheet but living, breathing people of flesh and blood, he would think twice about selling what was their heritage as well as hers. Kyle remembered the American publisher and his English wife who had been mentioned as potential buyers, and she shivered.

But it was a different sort of tremor that ran through her as Fier turned sharply and she was thrown briefly against him. She caught hold of the padded grab handle in the door and pulled herself away. 'This isn't the way back to Dovercourt!'

'I know.' In jeans and a high-necked black sweater, he glanced across at her. 'But I noticed a pub down here when we came past earlier. I thought we'd stop for lunch.'

'But. . . .' Kyle began, and stopped. What point was there in arguing? He must know as well as she did that Grace would be expecting them. What point was there in starting a discussion about something he had already decided? Besides, Fier would never argue. The thought flashed across her mind. Fier would just assume that he got his way.

A part of her was also pleased that the morning was going to continue. She had been reluctant to go with him at first—reluctant and more than a little apprehensive—but, like the tenants and their families, she too had been caught up in the enormous charm he could exercise when he chose. She had, she realised to her surprise, enjoyed the morning. She had enjoyed answering questions that tested her deep knowledge of the estate to its limit and she had lost her usual inhibition and reserve in her sense of first, Fier's evident surprise and then his acceptance of her as a highly competent person in her own right.

There was colour in her cheeks and some of the sherry-flecked brown hair she could see reflected in the car's wing mirror had escaped from its neat pleat to form a windblown haze of curls and tendrils around her face and neck. She looked younger, somehow, and lighthearted. She certainly felt more lighthearted than she had since she had heard of her father's death.

The car park of the half-timbered Tudor public house was crowded and so was the single bar. It was close to Chichester and on fine days such as this, office workers would steal an hour to add to their usual one and drive out to lunch. The bar was full of laughing, talking people, but just as they went in, a man and a woman got up from a small corner table and Fier guided her across to it.

'The power of positive thinking!' He acknowledged her surprise at their good luck. He also looked younger, somehow, and more relaxed, but she still had no idea what thoughts were passing under the brilliant cobalt surface of his eyes. 'Take it for granted that you'll get what you've set your heart on,' he explained, 'and it will very probably come true.'

Did that mean just an empty table in a crowded bar or a buyer for Dovercourt? Kyle felt herself begin to tense, and some of her tension must have communicated itself to the fingers lightly underneath her elbow, because they abruptly dropped away. 'What do you want to eat and drink?' The face which had earlier been smiling and relaxed was now tight and hard.

'Oh, I don't know.' She looked away. 'Anything will do.' The day which had started off so well was, after all, going to turn out as badly as she had feared.

'Will you please stop doing that?' When he spoke, his vehemence startled her.

'What?' She forgot and looked straight up at him. 'Doing what?' she faltered.

'Being so obliging and self-effacing that it hurts!' he snapped. 'You're a woman, not a piece of wallpaper, so try not to fade into it!'

She flushed. Old habits died hard, but how was he to know that?

'Now,' he said with weary patience, 'let's start again. What would you like to eat and drink?'

'A lemonade shandy and a sandwich. Any sort——' it was out before she caught it. 'Ham,' she substituted quickly. 'But let me come and help.'

He shot her a glance that stopped her. 'Sit!' he ordered. 'I can doubtless manage!'

What had gone wrong? Mortified and embarrassed, sure that the people at the next table had overheard them, Kyle sat and watched the dark head and shoulders part the crowds and make an easy pathway to the packed bar. For a while there had been companionship—even the possibility of friendship—as they had driven along the winding Sussex lanes in their riot of full summer leaf. She had even forgotten her usual inhibitions in the impersonal mental exercise of answering his steady stream of questions about the workings of the estate.

At least Grace had been right in one thing—Kyle pushed the other outrageous suggestion about marriage to one side—if Dovercourt was taken from them, she could always find work as a secretary.

It was ironic, really. She remembered the number of times she had sat in the small, dark office on the ground floor of the house and raged against the unfairness that had made Grace the favoured daughter and left her, hardly noticed, on the outside. And yet now it was she who had the skills to make a living—the book-keeping and the typing she had been forced to teach herself— whereas Grace had no means of support. Except her beauty! Grace might not have their mother's gift as an actress or their mother's total disregard for the conventions, but in looks she was most certainly Thea's daughter.

Thea had once pulled strings to get Grace a small part in the post-London tour of one of her West End plays. Grace had been in the hiatus between her two marriages and that had been when Alexei had seen her. He had gone to the play one night and, after that, he had followed the tour from town to town with the single-mindedness of the obsessed. His pursuit had ended when Grace's divorce from Philip had been finalised and she had said yes to his proposal. But the marriage had ended almost before it had begun, Grace spoiled and wilful and Alex uncertain when to give in or to apply the reins.

But there would be other men and other marriages. Unlike Thea, Grace would not have affairs. Kyle tried to envy her, but passion of the sort Grace—and Thea— inspired seemed to have the quality of a Roman candle; burning fiercely and then leaving cold dead ashes.

She wondered what it would be like to be in love. There had been someone once—a young partner with the firm of lawyers that had dealt with Dovercourt's business for generations. With hindsight, Kyle realised that he had pursued her, but she had neither realised nor responded at the time and, coming up against the wall of her natural reticence, he had not persisted. Some day, perhaps, there would be a husband and a family—but she was the quiet one, the satellite in the background of other, more brilliant suns. A self-effacing strip of wallpaper: she now had another description of herself!

Sitting at the table in the crowded bar, she tried but failed to visualise that young solicitor's face.

'Here you are!' Another face, one it would be much more difficult to forget, bent over her as Fier deposited two glasses and an oval wooden platter loaded with sandwiches on the table. As he did so, a tweedy type behind him moved aside and, past his shoulder, Kyle could see the barmaid, totally indifferent to the clamour going on around her, gazing down the narrow corridor with a bemused expression on her face. At least someone envied her, but then the barmaid didn't know she wasn't there by choice—Fier's choice. She was there instead of Grace.

The gap behind Fier closed and the barmaid disappeared behind a sea of heads and shoulders. Fier sat down and suddenly there were no crowds, just a man with a chiselled, arrogant face sitting opposite.

'There was no ham, so I got beef and cheese.' He pushed the garnished wooden platter closer. 'Which do you want?'

'It doesn't matter,' she replied automatically.

He turned his wrist and glanced at the wafer-thin gold Cartier watch. 'Five minutes!' he said abruptly.

'I'm sorry?' She stopped with an unidentified sandwich quarter half way to her mouth.

'Five minutes ago, I had you starting to behave like a reasonably confident human being. Now we're back to square one again! What the hell's wrong with you?' He was angry, suddenly—really angry.

Kyle felt a stir of anger of her own. His attack was taking her totally by surprise. If she had thought anything, she had thought this unexpected lunch was designed to discuss what they had seen and done that morning without having to bore Grace with estate business, but now, it seemed, she was to be the one dissected under the icy blue microscope of his eyes. 'I'm sorry if I don't please you!' she retorted stiffly.

'You don't!' He was quite blunt. 'You've got a good mind, a good figure, lovely legs and an unusual face, but instead of putting them together and using them, you go round behaving like a second class citizen! Is that what you want, Kyle?' If it hadn't been for the crowds around them, she had the shrewd suspicion that he would have leaned across and gripped her chin and forced her to meet him face to face. 'That everyone should take you at your own estimation of yourself?'

'Well, what else do you expect?' Was that really her, answering back so forcefully? She had never spoken to anyone like that in her life, but the knot of tight control inside her had come undone. 'From the moment we heard that Ash—my father,' she stumbled slightly, 'had died, we also heard nothing except the name Fier Cailloux. Fier Cailloux was going to inherit Dovercourt! It was up to Fier Cailloux what was going to happen next. All we could do was sit and wait! And you accuse me of behaving like a second class citizen!' She heard her voice rise and crack. 'How else would any woman feel?'

'That's better!' She had expected anything except

approval, but an approving smile now crossed his face. 'Some fire at last! One day we might even get you to look like someone other than the family housekeeper!'

The shot went home. 'If you wanted glamour, you should have lunched with Grace!' Kyle responded shortly. 'That's more her style!'

'I'd noticed.' The smile went knowing. 'Wake up, Kyle! Live! If you go round behaving like a slave that's exactly how people are going to treat you.' The crowded bar was still there, but now he leaned across and brushed a strand of errant hair back from her forehead. 'You're an intelligent, attractive woman. Why not behave like one?'

'How I behave is entirely my affair!' She could feel the light touch of his fingers long after he had taken them away.

'Is it?' A raised black eyebrow over a pair of knowing eyes made her suddenly remember Grace's extravagant suggestion that she should be his wife, and the quick rush of colour underneath her skin was reflected in the sudden gleam of knowledge dancing in those eyes. 'Tell me,' he switched the subject, 'what do *you* want? Not Grace——' he forestalled her with a raised hand, '—or Thea—not the glittering Haultain women everyone knows so much about, but you—Kyle Haultain,' he paused. 'The beautiful Haultain woman in the background of them all. What do you want, Kyle?'

He was suddenly deadly serious, and suddenly, so was she. By provoking her to the point where she almost lost control, he had made her feel an individual. For the first time in her life, a man was seeing her not as an extension of Grace or Thea but totally and utterly as herself. And, what was more, he was asking her opinion as if it was the most important one. It was ludicrous, of course. The moment he set eyes on Grace again, Fier would realise that. It was what Grace and Thea wanted that would count, as it had always done— No! She stopped. It was what Fier had already decided in a mind she could not read that was what eventually would take place, but she still put all the conviction she could muster into her quiet reply. 'I want Dovercourt to stay just as it is.' And I want to marry you! The words exploded in her head. 'And I would like another drink.' She held out her glass in a suddenly trembling hand.

'. . . I suppose their marriage was really over long before Ash died. It just suited them to keep up appearances.' It must be the gin, the large gin, that she had asked for and Fier had brought back and put firmly on the table in front of her that was making her so talkative. She never smoked and rarely drank and it had been sheer panic that had made her ask for it. What a time and what a place—Kyle glanced around the by now half empty bar—to discover that her assumption that she could never fall in love had, like so much else in her life, been something that Thea and Grace had decided for her. Not that she was in love, of course. She scarcely knew him. You couldn't fall in love with an almost-stranger, no matter what the songs might say. It was Grace with her preposterous suggestion about marriage who was to blame.

She glanced at the by now familiar figure through her lashes as he went on questioning her about her family. His head, with the fine bone structure under the brown skin, could have been carved out of mahogany, except that no sculptor could reproduce the innate intelligence or the deep compelling blue of those cobalt eyes.

'Were you close to your father?' Under the lock of thick dark hair that had once more fallen across his forehead, those eyes were fixed on her.

'No, not very.' Kyle reached out and turned her glass slowly by its stem. 'I'd only seen him twice in the five years before he died.' And her grieving over losing him had been done long before. Perhaps when she realised that, as far as Ash Haultain was concerned, he only had one daughter. Or perhaps it had been when the last of a long line of browbeaten and dispirited governesses had finally given in her notice and Ash had materialised from the archaeological excavations that were his life and taken Grace away.

Philip Hagib had been Ash's young Lebanese assistant on that particular dig and, six months after Ash had arrived back in Kenya with his beautiful young daughter, Grace and Philip had eloped.

So Ash had lost and so had Grace and so had Philip. Their ill-considered marriage had lasted just one year. And as for Thea—it must be the unaccustomed alcohol that was making her look at her family so dispassionately, Kyle decided—everyone knew of Thea Robertson and her succession of thinly disguised young lovers.

'Mother's in a play in London now,' she explained. 'Otherwise she would have been here.'

She said it, but inwardly she doubted. Even if Thea had been 'resting', it was unlikely that she could have borne to drag herself away from London, no matter what the cause. As it was, Thea had the excuse of work to keep her away. The vogue for period revivals had come just when her age and her stylised form of acting had caused her career to flag, but both Wilde and Pinero might have written with Thea Robertson in mind and now she was appearing in a short, highly star-studded run of a Shaw comedy, more beautiful and more sought after than ever.

'And which parent do you take after?' His question brought all her new awareness of herself prickling to the surface of her skin.

'Neither, I suppose.' She sipped her drink in an effort to avoid him. 'Or maybe both.' She had her father's soft brown hair and his eyes, too, except that a touch of Thea's gold turned them into sherry. Her slim, high-breasted figure and her long legs came straight from Thea—Thea's acting style might age, but her figure was still that of a young girl—and the face that Fier had so foolishly called beautiful was totally her own. It was Grace who was entirely Thea, with her blonde hair and striking violet eyes and pink and white complexion. There was nothing of Ash Haultain in his favourite daughter. 'And you? Tell me about you?' It really must be the alcohol that was making her so reckless. To prove it, she took another sip and the gin-spiked tonic fizzled in her nose. 'You said you owned the wilderness.'

'Not all of it,' Fier smiled, 'but a part. The last part!'

It was something she had noticed without realising that she had, but when he talked about his home, it wasn't just his face that changed, it was his voice. It grew harsher, more alien. It was as if the easy intonation of the French Canadian part of him was stripped away to disclose the harder cadence of a much older tongue. Part French, part English but also part Cree and Iroquois. The Indian blood was there in the spare moulding of the faces and bones; the European heritage in the easy way he wore his expensive clothes. Kyle let her eyes drift over the black sweater as he began to talk, registering the contrast of hard muscle underneath soft cashmere and the way fine black hairs disappeared up underneath the ribbing at the wrist.

'My grandfather ran around the land I own.' His voice forced her to listen. 'It was a wager, a drunken bet.' The thin lips pinched. 'Two young members of the English aristocracy sent out to the Colonies with nothing better to do than lay odds on how far an Indian could run in seven days. What they forgot—or didn't consider it important enough to remember—was that the course they set was over the old burial and hunting grounds that had been taken from his people. They told the Indian he could keep the land he covered, so he didn't run for seven days. He ran for seven nights as well.' The nostrils flared with pride. Fier meant proud, Kyle suddenly remembered, and every ounce of it was visible. 'One of those young Englishmen was called Haultain,' he finished quietly. 'A generation later, the Indian's son married his daughter.'

And now another circle had been completed, Kyle thought confusedly. Another generation and now another son and a daughter from the English branch of that same family were sitting facing one another in an English country pub. And the Indian boy who had been the winner of that first wager still had the advantage; his grandson now not only owned the land that he had covered, he owned Dovercourt as well.

Looking at the carved face opposite—more Indian than European—her earlier sense of optimism died and a feeling of defeat ran through her. If it came to a choice between keeping Faucon d'Or or Dovercourt, could she really be in any doubt which one Fier would choose?

'It's time we went.' He was already standing and the bar, she noticed suddenly, was almost empty. Except for two men in one corner and the girl behind the counter with her eyes fixed longingly on Fier, they were the only ones left.

She got up, avoiding the hand that came out to help her round the table and seeing the quick flash of irritation on Fier's face. What a fool she had been to think that anything that had happened that morning could really make any difference. When it came to loyalties, she and Fier were hopelessly opposed.

They drove home in silence between a hazy blur of hedgerows, but Grace's face was anything but hazy when she met them at the door. It was an accusing mask of anger and she held Kyle well back behind Fier as they walked across the black and white tiled hall.

'You're drunk!' she snapped accusingly. 'And where the hell have you been?'

She had been on a roller-coaster of emotion, Kyle thought disjointedly. She wasn't drunk, but she had been led first to hope and then to disappointment about the future of Dovercourt and, most alarmingly of all, her feelings about herself had been shaken up and rearranged by the man now striding fluidly ahead of them.

She was not the same Kyle Haultain she had been when she had left, but the new feeling of self-confidence Fier had given her would be the last thing which would interest Grace. Her preoccupation was making up lost time with Fier. Compared to that, everything—even the prospect of losing Dovercourt—was secondary.

'And how's your headache?' From his vantage point

beside the library window, Fier put the question drily.

'My——?' Grace had forgotten and her fine gold brows momentarily drew into a puzzled line. 'Oh, that!' Her face cleared. 'It's fine . . . I mean, it's gone.' She smiled up at him, as fair as he was dark and completely free of guile. 'And how was your morning? You've been gone so long, I thought you were never coming back, so you must have seen everything! Have you decided anything yet? About Dovercourt, I mean?' she prompted.

'Yes.' For Grace there was a long, indulgent look, but for Kyle the room went dead and her stomach did a somersault. This was it. The moment they had been waiting for after months of uncertainty. In just a few seconds now, they would know where their future lay. 'I've decided I ought to meet your mother. Why don't we drive up to town and see her play tonight?'

Kyle was still groping for some underlying meaning to what her ears told her he had said long after Grace's enthusiastic acceptance had died away. She had steeled herself to hear about the future; instead she was listening to plans for going up to London and meeting Thea. It didn't make sense—but yes, of course it did. No man in his right senses would ignore an opportunity of meeting Thea Robertson. Kyle's tenuous sense of confidence began to wane. After a morning spent in the company of the unattractive one—the diffident, self-effacing, second class citizen!—what man would pass by a chance of meeting the second of the two beautiful Haultain woman?

'We'll leave at six,' she heard him say. 'Can you be ready?' It would have been to Grace, still smiling up at him, but the question and the look were aimed at Kyle.

Grace's face dropped. 'Is Kyle coming with us, then?' She sounded disappointed.

'Of course.' The level cobalt eyes stayed fixed on Kyle.

'No, it's fine.' She turned away from them, confused. 'I'll stay here . . . I've got a lot to do. Besides, what about the car?' She caught sight of the parked Mercedes on the gravelled drive. 'There's only room in it for two.'

She didn't want to go. Didn't want to be with Grace and Thea and have Fier see her for what she really was. He might have called her self-effacing, but he had also said she was attractive, Kyle remembered suddenly. And attractive was only a short step from beautiful. But if he saw her with both Grace and Thea, he would realise what a hopeless hope that was.

'There you are, then!' Grace sounded satisfied. 'We can hardly turn up at a theatre in the Land Rover!'

'I'll rent a car.' He was angry, not with Grace, but Kyle, and she was once more totally mystified. 'And you,' he added forcefully, 'are coming with us!'

Grace and Fier were in the garden when the delivery van arrived. Kyle could hear Grace's voice—sharp suddenly and excited—through the open window, and then, a few seconds later, she heard the sound of Fernanda's slippers coming along the corridor towards her room.

'Señora!' Fernanda knocked on the door and pushed it open. She was carrying a box, a large white cardboard box, with the name of a Brighton boutique scrolled over it. 'This come for you!' She laid it on the bed.

Kyle frowned across. 'What is it?' she asked doubtfully.

Fernanda shrugged and spread her hands. They were here pursuing Manuel's dream of opening a hotel; she didn't have to bother with this curious northern language. Apart from a few odd words, made even more difficult to understand by a thick Catalan accent,—Fernanda Seguera relied on mime and dumb show.

Kyle went across and opened the white box. There was tissue paper inside, then more tissue paper, and she finally lifted out a long black dress. There was no card.

'Fernanda, who sent this?' she asked more out of amazement than any expectation of a reply and, true to her expectation, Fernanda just shrugged and smiled encouragingly before she left the room.

It must be Thea, Kyle decided, lifting the dress and holding it against her. It was the sort of quixotic, impulsive gesture she would make. No word for months, no sign of interest for years and then an expensive—very expensive—present in a fit of guilty conscience. Kyle went back to the box and hunted for a card, holding the dress in one hand and unconsciously rubbing the soft silk against her cheek. She had been right the first time. There was no card, but the dress was definitely Thea! Low-cut, with an extravagant frilling around the strapless bodice and down the side of the side-slit skirt—and black. On Thea, black looked fabulous, but Kyle had never worn it in her life. Black and brown just didn't go; she had learned the maxim just as soon as she had learned that she had plain brown hair.

The remarkable thing about the incident was Thea's timing. It was almost as if she had known they were going to the theatre. Tempted, Kyle again took the dress across to the long, slightly cloudy mirror and held it up against her. Another person looked back at her, softly focused in the misty glass; familiar but not quite someone she really knew. This other person had gold flecks in her eyes which made them deeper and more mysterious and the soft sheen of the ebony silk found highlights that turned her hair to copper. The only part of this almost stranger that looked drab and dull were the shoulders in their pale cream blouse, almost the colour of the one evening dress Kyle had hanging in her wardrobe.

She could never wear this dress, of course. It was far too daringly cut and outrageous, but—it wouldn't hurt to try it on! Kyle laid the dress down gently on her bed and began to take off her blouse.

The woman who gazed back at her for a few brief moments from the mirror had golden shoulders and a long slim neck. Between taking off her skirt and blouse and slipping on the dress, Kyle had piled her hair up on to her head in a soft Victorian-style crown, and the face beneath that crown was slightly tilted on one side, regarding itself with deep coquettish eyes.

And that was exactly what that dress was, Kyle decided, reaching for the zip and sliding it carefully down her back. It was a dress for a coquette—someone confident of her ability and power to charm with its low, low neckline and the fullish side-slit skirt that had been designed to give a tantalising glimpse of a long, slender leg. She would thank Thea, of course, for her present when she saw her later—but she couldn't possibly wear it. This new image of herself was frightening.

The only part of the new image that had survived when she went downstairs was the hairstyle. She had taken the bulk of her fine hair and secured it firmly but softly on her head so that tendrils, baby-soft and silky brown from her shower, framed her face and wisped gently around her neck. The rest of her was cream; cream and sensible in a boat-necked, short-sleeved taffeta dinner dress.

'Why aren't you dressed? We'll be leaving in a moment.' Fier caught sight of her from the library. She had seen him through the open door when she had been coming down the stairs, standing broodingly in front of the long window looking out across the lawn. She had wondered what he was thinking. Nothing pleasant by the look of him, but whatever it was, it had absorbed him so totally that he didn't hear her until she had almost reached the door and his failure gave her a second to collect herself, but even so, she was still not totally prepared for her reaction to her first sight of him when he finally caught the sound of her gold sandals on the black and white tiled hall floor and abruptly swung to face her.

He moved easily, swivelling lightly on his feet. Above the snowy brilliance of his ruffled shirt, his face was dark, shot with two pools of cobalt blue, and his hair intensified the blackness of his dinner jacket, not the other way around. He was powerful and he was foreign, turning the pastel light of an early English summer evening into something alien, and as he spoke, he moved towards her, his facial muscles tense, his mouth a hard, straight line. He was angry. For some reason, he was still angry.

'I asked why you hadn't changed.' His eyes took in the taffeta dress without a movement.

He hadn't noticed. 'But I have!' Suddenly nervous, Kyle ran her tongue across her lips.

'Yes, I can see that,' he said impatiently. 'But why aren't you wearing . . .?'

'*You* sent it!' A mystery became blindingly obvious. Diffident, self-effacing; she heard the words again, curt and clipped against a background of lunchtime pub conversation. How could she have forgotten? Of course Thea hadn't sent the dress now hanging in her wardrobe. It was Fier.

'Of course!' He now confirmed it.

'But how did you know . . . I mean. . . .' Another thought had struck her, a much more alarming one, and she looked away, conscious of his eyes upon her. How had he known her size? The body-hugging dress fitted perfectly. He had not only been studying her over lunch, but he had been doing it in a much more intimate way than she had realised. Colour spiralled up from the neckline of the cream taffeta to stain her neck and cheeks.

'How did I know your size?' He finished the question for her with an ironic smile and then went on to answer it. 'I may live in a wilderness, but you're not the first woman I've ever seen!'

Kyle was sure of it. Women would be drawn to Fier Cailloux no matter where he lived. She had seen Grace's reaction to him—and his to her. She had also felt her own response to Grace's wild idea that she should marry him.

'And now we've got that settled,' he said quietly, 'you'd better go and change. You've got five minutes.' He was close, much much too close. She could see the faint grain of his beard and feel the vibration of his voice in the air against her cheek.

'Oh, but I can't!' She said it at a point somewhere between his bow tie and his chin. 'I couldn't possibly accept a gift like that!' She couldn't possibly wear a dress that left her arms and shoulders naked and her breasts barely covered by the ruffled bodice.

'Why not?' He didn't bother to hide his derision. 'Are you afraid it might make people notice you? Isn't it about time you grew out of this false modesty and stopped hiding behind your sister's shadow?'

'That had nothing to do with it!' But had it? Was that really what she wanted? To be ignored—and safe. 'It's just that I can't possibly accept a present like that from a man, that's all,' she said instead.

'Oh, for God's sake, Kyle, I'm getting tired of this!' His temper escalated towards breaking point. 'Tell yourself it's from your cousin—tell yourself anything— but you'll go upstairs and get out of that apology for female fashion and get changed. You have five minutes!'

'No!' Cousin or not—and there was certainly nothing cousin-like about him at that moment—he had no right to order her about like this. She tilted her head right back and faced him. 'I'm either going as I am or not at all!'

'Then we'll have to see what we can do to make you change your mind, shan't we?' The silky softness of his voice should have been a warning. It was so much at odds with the sheer determination blazing in his eyes. But before she had a chance to guess what he intended, his hand was at her neck and she heard the stitching of the cream silk taffeta begin to crack.

'What are you doing?' She tried to fight him. 'Fier, stop!'

'When you decide to be less of an utter fool,' he answered quietly. A few more stitches parted company and the skin beneath his fingers began to burn. 'Do you want me to go on?' His eyes released her and dropped to her bare shoulder.

'No!' Her heart was pounding in her chest and when he finally let her go, she clutched the torn dress to her as she turned desperately away.

'Remember, Kyle!' His voice followed her wild flight across the hall and up the stairs. 'You have *four* minutes!'

CHAPTER THREE

'MISS ROBERTSON says to go on through. It's the first door on the left.' The stage door keeper put down the phone and barely looked at them.

But the man hurrying down the narrow backstage corridor towards them, still throwing on a raincoat, certainly did. And what man wouldn't? Kyle realised. Grace almost incandescent in pink silk with a crown of blush pink camellias in her blonde hair and, behind her, a perfect foil, a taller girl in black. The man stopped and stood back against the dirty cream-painted wall to let them pass.

'Paul! How lovely!' Grace recognised him and paused. 'You were wonderful tonight!'

'Really?' The most famous eyebrow in the English-speaking theatre wryly lifted, but the eyes went across Grace's shoulder and fastened on to Kyle.

'You know my sister, don't you?' Grace caught their direction and turned slightly fretfully. Men weren't supposed to look at other women when she was there. 'You've met Kyle?'

'No, I don't think I have.' The hand that, five minutes earlier, had been linked with Thea's as they stood centre stage taking enthusiastic curtain calls now took Kyle's in firm, warm fingers and the most recent of a distinguished line to play Shaw's King Magnus looked at her approvingly. They had met, of course, just as Kyle had met most of Thea's leading men, but it was hardly surprising that he failed to associate the rather shadowy brown-haired girl who stayed firmly in the background with this woman in the seductively low-cut dress.

'But you haven't met our cousin, Fier Cailloux.' Grace broke the moment by moving slightly and sliding her arm possessively through Fier's. 'He's here from Canada.'

A conversation started between the three of them; Kyle slipped back into anonymity and she was glad of it. Until the dimming of the theatre lights, she had felt hopelessly conspicuous all evening; it was a relief to be once more overlooked.

The car Fier had ordered to bring them to London had been chauffeur-driven—here was money, Grace's eyes had registered when she had seen it. Money over and above what was needed to keep Dovercourt. That had been embarrassing enough, but what was worse was that Fier had sat with them in the back, his long legs in the jump seat facing them occasionally and disturbingly brushing up against hers. Grace had done the talking, keeping his attention almost exclusively, but even so, Kyle had been aware that his eyes had slid across to her far more often than was necessary. She had seen the glint that lit them and felt his inner smile as he registered the soft gleam of her bare shoulders against the leather seat and the first curve of her swelling breasts rising from the black ruffle of the disputed dress.

At least her legs were hidden. The slit skirt had fallen apart when she had got into the limousine and she had quickly wrapped it around her legs when she had sat down.

That was the first time she had seen that quiet private smile and, although the car was air-conditioned, she felt flushed.

The dress had marked the end of the first round of a confrontation that she was determined was not going to go on. In itself, the incident had been trivial—especially in the light of Fier's gift to Grace—but Fier had won, just, she suspected, as he would win in any clash of wills no matter how trivial the issue. He stood there now, dominating the theatre's narrow backstage corridor.

'Goodnight, Miss Haultain. I can see that I must try and persuade my co-star to invite both her lovely daughters backstage more often!' It was an actor's compliment, made as the conversation going on beside her finished and the speaker continued his interrupted way to the stage door and the last bus home to his wife and family, but that didn't stop Grace's face hardening for a moment under the coronet of fresh camellias nestling in her hair. She was the lovely daughter in the family.

'Come on,' she ordered brusquely, 'let's go. Mother will be waiting.'

Fier made no comment. It was his quiet amusement as they walked on in single file towards Thea's dressing room that made Kyle's shoulders burn. Not quite a round, but somehow, he had won another point.

It wasn't until Grace had tapped on the door beside the tarnished star and opened it that the burning feeling stopped. But then could anyone have eyes for anything except their first sight of Thea Robertson?

'Darling! Come in!' Thea was relaxing on the opulent chaise-longue that her contract stipulated for every dressing room she occupied. One hand held a half full glass of champagne and the skin of the softly rounded arm was milky white against the flowing dark blue draperies of a Grecian-style costume. Another clause in Thea Robertson's contracts; her costumes were always designer-made. This one came from Paris. But it wasn't the dress or the flawless skin or the beautiful heart-shaped face that made the first, incredible impression, it was the whole and total Thea, seen against a background of massed flowers and reflected and re-reflected in the surrounding floor-to-ceiling mirrors. The brilliant lights around the make-up mirror had been switched off; the room was softly lit and it was Cleopatra, Josephine and Mata Hari who lay there watching them, if—that was—any of those great courtesans had had Thea's fabulous spun gold crown of hair.

No wonder she heard the quick intake of Fier's breath behind her! She was used to Thea, but even Kyle had caught her breath.

'Darling, you were wonderful?' Grace hurried across and laid her soft cheek against Thea's so that a second beautiful woman appeared in the surrounding mirrors.

'Was I?' Thea sounded surprised. 'I thought I was a little strained!' She suddenly caught sight of Fier and looked across, questioning.

'You were superb, Miss Robertson!' He took his cue and walked past Kyle towards her; a dark image in the mirrors.

'Nice to hear, but not quite true.' Thea looked up at him. 'As, I suspect, you very well know,' she added drily. 'Like any other woman, I'm always pleased to have compliments, but not when the eyes of the person paying them are telling a different tale!'

'Then let's just say you were very good then, shall we?' Kyle heard the wry note of new respect in Fier's voice.

'Yes, let's just say that.' Thea didn't take her remarkable violet eyes away from him. 'And who is this appallingly honest young man you've brought to plague me?' she asked Grace.

'Mother, this is Fier Cailloux. . . .'

'Alethea's son,' Thea interrupted. 'Yes,' she smiled, 'you would be. Your mother always did have good taste in men, which presumably is why she turned down a chance of marrying Ash,' she added bluntly. 'Just think—if she hadn't, we shouldn't have had all these problems! And I assume she took pains to make sure her one and only child looked just like his father. Just like Alethea, doing deals with the Almighty to get just what she wanted! And you do look just like your father, I presume?' she added sharply.

'Except for the eyes,' Fier pointed out, amused.

'Yes. . . .' Thea had suddenly become pensive. 'Always except for the eyes! And now, my dears,' it seemed to be an effort for her to slip back into her usual brittle self, 'where are we going? I have this tiresome young man waiting for me at Gerry's, so if——' she suddenly broke off. 'But who's that?' She peered at Kyle still standing in the doorway; no more than a shadowy outline without the glasses Thea was too vain to wear in company.

'It's me, Mother.' Kyle obediently moved forward to become a fourth image in the mirrors; two golden women and a third with amber hair and eyes, all dominated by the figure of the man who towered over them.

'Kyle?' There was no mistaking Thea's incredulity. 'It can't be—I don't believe it! What have you done to yourself?'

'Don't you like it?' Her neck and shoulders felt

terribly exposed and she instinctively put a hand to her bare throat.

'It's not that I don't like it,' Thea said doubtfully. 'It's just that you look so——'

'Different,' Fier cut in firmly. 'We decided that tonight was the night for your elder daughter to take the town by storm!'

'And I must say you've succeeded!' Thea drawled, shooting him a sideways glance. 'I didn't even recognise my own child!'

'But look what Fier gave me!' Bored with her unusual position on the outskirts of a conversation concerning another woman, Grace broke in eagerly, bending her head with its crown of flowers for Thea's admiration. 'No one has *ever* given me camellias!'

Which was why it had been so much easier to accept the dress. Not that she had been given any choice, but when Kyle had come selfconsciously down the stairs with the black silk rustling seductively around her, the first thing she had seen through the open library doorway had been Fier gently pinning his floral tribute into Grace's hair. She had thought—heaven only knew what she had thought to account for Fier's outrageous gift to her—but the moment she caught sight of Grace's flowers, it all slipped into place.

The dress was something to transform an ugly duckling into a swan, at least for a night. Or perhaps turning a housekeeper into a house guest would be a better simile. Kyle remembered his automatic assumption of her place at Dovercourt when they had met. But his gift to Grace was a fitting compliment to what she already was. Beautiful, enchanting, capable of inspiring a mindless adoration in any man she met. She would not have thought Fier was the type of man to be so easily enslaved, but then appearances were deceptive. Kyle contrasted the dark strength of the head she could see in front of her with Grace's fragile beauty. The pity of it was that Grace wasn't free to marry him. If she had been, Dovercourt would not have been in its present jeopardy.

They had heard her then and turned, and Grace's eyes had widened as they had seen the extravagant black dress. Fier, too, had looked at her with an expression of satisfaction on his carved face. And he could afford to be satisfied, Kyle had thought cynically. With Grace's pale shoulders inches in front of him, rising from the rose silk of her St Laurent gown and her blonde head crowned, not with vine leaves, but with his tribute of blush pink camellias, Fier had more than provided a foil of darkness for the beautiful Haultain sister's golden beauty. For the first time in her life, Kyle had felt truly jealous of her sister.

'Darling, I'm afraid I've got a small apology to make!' In the flower-filled dressing room, Thea's voice claimed Kyle's attention. Thea never apologised and even though the explanation wasn't meant for her, the occasion was unique enough to make Kyle prick up her ears. 'When I got your message that you were coming tonight, I did something I probably shouldn't have done—I called Alex.'

'You what?' Grace was appalled, but something made Kyle look swiftly across at Fier. His face was unreadable.

'I called Alex,' Thea was repeating. 'And I suggested he meet us here.'

'Mother, how could you do such a thing?'

'Darling . . .' Thea was warning, 'you can't go through life collecting broken marriages. Philip's over

and done with. There's nothing we can do about that
and you probably shouldn't have married him in the
first place——' Now Kyle saw Fier react: an almost
imperceptible flick of cobalt eyes from Thea to Grace.
He was learning something that even he hadn't known.
'——and you couldn't have done if it hadn't been for
that fool father of yours,' Thea continued forcibly.
'Taking a sixteen-year-old girl off into the wilds of
Africa and then being absolutely shattered when she
runs off with the first attractive man she meets. But
Alex is different. He loves you—yes, Grace, he does!'
She overrode Grace's fierce denial. 'And you haven't
given him, or your marriage, a chance. Anyway,' Thea
showed the toughness behind the porcelaine façade,
'I've invited him, and you'll at least try and be pleasant.' The reproduction old-fashioned ivory telephone
on the table beside her shoulder began to ring. 'That's
probably the stage door now to tell me he's arrived.'

Alexei Orsinski's footsteps echoing down the passageway brought another sort of tension into the over-
heated dressing room. He stood, stiff-legged and hos-
tile as he was introduced to Fier and then immediately
circled warily towards Grace, like a large, blond dog
sensing a threat to its territory.

'Grace!' His handsome face lit up.

'Alex.' Grace barely acknowledged him.

The acknowledgement came from Fier; Kyle saw
him watching the interchange with narrowed eyes.
What was he thinking now? she wondered. Nothing
pleasant, judging from the expression on his face. He
had already had one shock; learning that Grace had
been married once before. What was he thinking about
the present situation?

'And now, my children,' in spite of an atmosphere

thick enough to cut with a knife, Thea sounded satisfied, 'it's time for us to leave.'

They went to Gerry's, a basement bar and supper club in Shaftesbury Avenue, at the centre of London's West End theatre world, where Thea's latest 'young man' was waiting. Looking at the floppy brown hair and the soft brown eyes watching Thea with a spaniel's adoration, Kyle found herself wondering what her mother's life might have been like if, instead of this young man or all the other equally nondescript ones who had gone before him, she had found someone she couldn't dominate. Someone who mastered her and not the other way around. A man like Fier, perhaps.

Kyle glanced at him and quickly glanced away. It was too late, and had been ever since Ash Haultain had given up the battle to control his beautiful and headstrong wife. Thea had reached the stage where she would never tolerate any man's control. Besides—Kyle watched her laughing up at her young man as they danced—Thea Robertson was happy, in her way.

The music pounded on at battleground proportions. They had come on from Gerry's to a supper club which offered dancing on a tiny crowded floor. Like Gerry's, this also had a largely show business clientele, so there had been no rush for autographs when the great Thea Robertson had arrived. In fact, for once—Kyle had noticed and had been amused—the great Thea Robertson, at home amongst her peers, hadn't even bothered to make her usual dramatic entrance.

Kyle wished someone would lower the decibel level of the frantic disco music and she also wished the strobing lights would stop, but most of all, she wished that an evening which had already gone on well into tomorrow would finally come to an end.

Alexei's arrival on the scene had changed them from five people into three pairs. Alexei, fiercely possessive, staying close to Grace, and Grace, although obviously inwardly rebellious, sufficiently in awe of Thea not to make a scene. They were dancing now; two fair heads, not hard to pick out even in the strobing lights that turned everything into the fast motion of a silent movie. Thea and Roger—or was it Mark?—were also easy to pick out; dancing a showy, heel-tapping sequence that had a circle of other, barely moving, dancers clapping hands and snapping fingers on the edge of the circle that had cleared itself around them.

Sitting there in the extravagant black dress, an untouched brandy glass beside her coffee cup, Kyle wished herself a million miles away. Thea's manoeuvre to get Grace and Alex back together had left her alone with Fier.

A dance with Thea, during which they had talked more than they danced with Thea's slim white arms linked lightly around his neck and her head bent slightly back as she listened, and then another, even shorter one with Grace with Alex watching every look and movement, and Fier had escorted Grace back to their table and sat down. He was sitting now, slightly apart with his chair pushed back and his long legs stretched out: a dark angel with watchful, hard blue eyes. He had not asked Kyle to dance.

The black dress made her feel conspicuous and a shiver ran along her spine when she turned back from her inspection of the dance floor to find him watching her.

'Are you cold?' It was hard to hear him above the pounding music.

'No.' She mouthed it rather than spoke and turned

selfconsciously away, fiddling with the short stem of her brandy glass.

He was as impatient to be gone as she was—and why not? The disco music changed to a slow, soft beat and she saw a reluctant Grace drawn into Alex's arms. The camellias were wilting now, she noticed, battered by heat and noise. No wonder the man who had given them was anxious to be gone. He had known about Alexei—Kyle remembered Grace telling him—but he hadn't known he would be there that night.

A tall man she half recognised stood up between her and the floor and started to thread his way around the tables towards her with a tentative, enquiring smile.

'Will you dance?' She hadn't heard or seen him move, but Fier was suddenly behind her chair. The man approaching her faltered and turned back.

'I'm afraid I don't.' She drew away from the out-stretched hand inches away from her bare shoulder.

'Then that makes two of us,' he answered smoothly. 'But I think we could manage this!'

The floor came towards them in slow motion. The only thing that was real was the touch of his hand above her elbow and, when he turned her to him, the convulsive movement of her entire body as she brushed against his thigh. Even the lights were a part of the conspiracy; soft now and muted to complement the quiet dreaminess of the music. His breath stirred the hair against her forehead and the hand that rested lightly on her naked back turned her skin to velvet. He led her easily, compelling her feet to fit in with the rhythm of the music and, when another couple veered towards them, he drew her to him. She couldn't breathe, but it didn't seem to matter. All that mattered was that her hands were somehow around his neck, their backs brushing against the crisp darkness of his hair and that his arms, through the thin silk of her dress, were holding her close to his chest.

They turned and Thea appeared behind his shoulder and, behind Thea, Grace. Grace was jealous, Kyle realised suddenly. She knew the look; the downward turn of the perfect mouth and the petulant expression on her face. Alexei obviously adored her, but that wasn't enough.

'How long has your sister been separated from her husband?' Reality came back like an icy plunge as Fier asked the question. He, too, had noticed Grace and Alex.

'Since the spring.' Her hands were no longer brushing against his hair and the inches he had put between them when he had bent his head to ask the question seemed like yards.

'And do they often see each other?' His question seemed dispassionate; Thea wasn't the only actor in the family.

'Not often.' Kyle wished the tight lump in her chest would dissolve. 'You saw Grace earlier,' she must be honest. Honesty was about the only thing that she had left. That, and the ability to type and keep books. 'She didn't know Mother had invited him tonight.'

'But they see each other as often as Orsinski can arrange it.' It was a statement, not a question.

'Yes, I suppose so.' She cleared her throat. 'Yes,' she repeated firmly, 'yes, they do.'

'And does Orsinski live in England?' The cobalt eyes were focussed above her head.

'Not really. His family came out of Russia in the Revolution. They have a house in Paris and a home in Cannes.'

'Ah, yes—the famous villa with the hunting trophies on the walls!' He had remembered; just as every man remembered everything about Grace. 'And they've been married . . .?' He left the question hanging in the music-impregnated air.

'Two years.' A wedding in the rites of the Russian Orthodox Church. Kyle had been there. The candles and the crowns held over two fair heads, and Grace's radiance. But there was no need to tell him that.

'But Orsinski's not her first husband?' The question came abruptly.

'No.' Why wouldn't he stop asking her about Grace? Did he really think she needed that to prove his interest? She stumbled awkwardly against his feet. 'I'm sorry,' she said, also awkwardly.

'Why be?' His eyes were luminous in the soft coloured light; they reminded Kyle of the lapis lazuli on one of the Orsinski collection of jewelled Fabergé eggs. 'I'm dancing with the most beautiful woman in the room, so why apologise?'

It was a meaningless compliment and he was mocking her. The next of his interminable questions proved it.

'Tell me,' he asked abruptly, 'if I sell Dovercourt, then what will happen?'

'To Grace, you mean?' It was a gratuitous comment; she knew it as she glanced up at his face. 'I don't know.' She shrugged her shoulders and felt the black silk slide along her naked back. 'She could perhaps go back to Alex.' The arms around her tightened, but it was only another couple dancing too close. 'Or perhaps Thea would make her an allowance and she could get a flat in London.'

'I see.' The arms relaxed. 'And you?' He changed

the subject alarmingly. 'If I sell Dovercourt, what will you do?'

'I'll manage.' Kyle drew pride around her bare shoulders like a cloak. 'I shall probably move to London and see if I can get an office job. I do have some ability, you know!'

'Ah, yes—the independent Miss Kyle Haultain!' His voice was suddenly more French than English; a caress that ran along her spine. They both had French blood in their ancestry; his mixed with Indian and hers from the long-dead knight who had come over with the Conqueror. 'Tell me,' the music stopped and his words hung clearly in the suddenly muted room, 'if Dovercourt is sold, do you think your sister will go back to her husband?'

'I don't care how much pressure Thea puts on me or how good for me Alex is supposed to be, I won't go back to him! I won't! I won't! It's my life and no one's going to tell me how to lead it!' Grace's lips quivered and her face, childlike without make-up in the early morning sunshine streaming into the breakfast room, had the silver stains of tears—real tears—running down her cheeks.

It had been well after three when they had finally got home from London. The day—Fier's last at Dovercourt—had already started badly and looked as if it was going to go on that way. At eight-thirty in the morning, Kyle already felt limp.

'No one's trying to force you to go back to Alex,' she said tiredly. 'It's just that Thea seems to think you should give your marriage a second chance.'

Try harder, was in fact what Thea had firmly said when the three of them had been left alone together in the powder room just before they left the supper club. Try harder and grow up, Thea had said crossly. Marriage wasn't a fairytale of living happily ever after. It needed work, and Grace would do well to realise that before she went on to make the second big mistake of her life.

'It's beyond me how she thinks she's got the right to tell me anything with the sort of life she leads!' Grace said moodily. 'She was the one who walked out on Father, after all, and that Roger Whatshisname she had trailing round behind her last night was the bitter end. How long does our dear mother think that little love affair is going to last, I wonder?' she went on spitefully. 'If she's so fond of dear Alex, I'm surprised she doesn't take him for herself. At least he's older than some of the men she's had!'

'Grace!' Kyle was shocked.

'Oh, I know, I know! One shouldn't believe half what one reads in the magazines!' Grace had the grace to look contrite. 'And I know she's only telling me for my own good—do what I say and not what I do, that sort of thing. But I *hate* people telling me things for my own good! Oh, I don't know!' Her mood changed and she sighed. 'If it was always like it was last night with Alex, then perhaps I would consider it——' she brightened. 'Did you notice how jealous he was of Fier?'

Yes, she had. Alex's face had almost bulged every time he looked at Fier. And she had also noticed how—if not jealous, at least how preoccupied Fier had been. Sitting slightly apart in his chair, his eyes resting broodingly first on one and then the other and then, when they had danced, his constant stream of questions about Grace's future.

The only time he had dropped his mask of wary speculation was when he had been dancing with Thea and they had been deep in private conversation. It seemed to have been a conversation that had pleased them both; at least, Thea was radiant and Fier was smiling with a brilliant flash of white when they had walked back to the table. Something had been settled to their mutual satisfaction, but whether it was the future of Dovercourt or something much more personal, neither of them was giving any hint.

Thea had swept off to her Mayfair flat with her young man in tow and Fier, like Kyle and Grace, had been virtually silent on the long drive home. But this morning he would have to tell them what he had decided about the estate. He was leaving that afternoon. In a few hours at most, not only Grace but she might be thinking in terms of a new and vastly different future. In spite of the sunny morning, Kyle suddenly felt chilly, and she reached across the breakfast room table for the coffee pot.

'You can make that two while you're at it.' Fier walked in while she was pouring. A nerve jumped in her hand and a splotch of coffee appeared on the white cloth.

'Of course.' She kept her eyes fixed on the small spreading stain while she pulled a second cup towards her and began to pour. It was difficult to keep a steady hand, and a pulse she never knew she had was beating in her throat. The thought of losing Dovercourt had always upset her, but never before like this.

He had a fawn cashmere sweater and pale cream pants and his throat was dark and bare. His hair was damp after his shower and she had seen comb tracks, but the one unruly black lock had already fallen across his forehead to give him his usual quizzical, buccaneering air. She had looked up for a second—no less than that—and yet every detail was etched on her mind's eye.

'What's wrong? You look upset.'

Kyle passed his coffee under cover of his questioning of Grace, careful not to let her eyes rise above the level of the strong-fingered hand that reached out and took it. The tiny black hairs on his wrist below the pushed-up sleeve of his sweater gleamed dully on his wrist.

'I am upset. Mother's bullying me!' There had been a subtle change in Grace's voice. Instead of petulance, she was forlorn, misunderstood and in need of help.

'Really? What about?' Kyle could hear the lifted eyebrow and imagine the concerned enquiry on his face. It had been there the previous night when they had been dancing and he had been questioning her about Grace.

Now, in her sweater and pale blue jeans, she might just as well not have been with them in the breakfast room. The black dress that had been responsible for even his slight amount of interest was in her wardrobe—out of sight, right at the back. She had worn it only once, and yet it already held too intolerable a memory of being held closely in his arms with the pulse beats of her body responding to those of his until, for one incredible moment, she had known what it was like to want a man and feel him wanting her. It had been illusory, of course. A crowded floor, preoccupation with something—someone—else, had all conspired to make him take her closely to him for this one 'duty' dance and hold her with his thigh brushing against hers and his hands possessively on her naked back.

She remembered her own hands clasped around his

neck, their backs just brushing the crispness of his hair, and she burned with embarrassment. The dress could go—to the local church jumble sale, to anything—she would never wear it again. Every time she caught sight of it, she would relive those moments, and then the next, when he had started questioning her about Grace and she had realised that, although his arms were round her, his thoughts were somewhere else.

'Mother's telling me I should go back to Alex!' Grace's tearful voice mingled with Kyle's thoughts.

At least she hadn't given herself away. At least Fier hadn't noticed any more than he would know about the self-destructive whim that had made her pass over an everyday cotton frock and, instead that morning, put on a pale blue sweater and a pair of even paler jeans. Grace's cast-offs, they were designer-made, of course, and they clung intimately to her hips and thighs. That black dress had a lot to answer for. And so did Grace, with her ridiculous idea that she should marry Fier.

Until then, she had been quite happy with her life. Now, nothing could ever be the same.

'And will you go back to him? To Orsinski?' An underlying urgency in Fier's question caught Kyle's ear. She didn't have to look up, but she did.

Fier's eyes were fixed on Grace as if more than just her future depended on her answer. It was the same question he had put to her the previous night when they had been dancing. The question Kyle had not been able to satisfy.

'No, never! Never in a million years!' Grace more than gave him his answer now—and she had never looked more beautiful. It was remarkable that she was up at all for breakfast and the lacy cuff of her white negligée framed her face like a frothing waterfall as she raised a hand dramatically to her forehead. 'I'd rather starve!'

No wonder Fier suddenly looked relaxed. Or, at least, no wonder a smile of quiet indulgence crinkled the corners of his eyes. 'I hardly think starving will be necessary,' he said drily, 'but now I know what your plans are, it certainly justifies my decision.'

He had decided what he was going to do about Dovercourt. The room went quiet. Even Grace was affected. The moment of truth had arrived; the moment that was going to decide their lives.

'I've decided against selling,' he said quietly. 'I'm still going back to Canada, but, for the time being at least, Dovercourt will stay exactly as it is.'

'Without making any changes?' Kyle was the first to find her voice. Fier glanced at her. Had she really been there all the time?

'Yes, one.' As she caught the note of resolution Kyle's heart sank. Dovercourt was going to stay the same, the Sullys and the Gibsons on their farms were safe, but she and Grace were going to have to leave. She had known the fleeting hope they weren't was too good to be true. And it was all because of Grace. Without Dovercourt and without Alex, Grace would only have one option left. She would have to turn to Fier. But Fier was going on. 'From now on, the extra money needed to run the estate will come from me, not Thea. Your mother will have no more financial responsibility for Dovercourt in any way, shape or form.'

'But——' Kyle paused and his eyes swivelled on to her. 'Does that mean that we can go on living here?'

'Of course!'

'And you're doing all this for nothing?' Grace sounded radiant. 'For absolutely nothing in return?'

'Oh, I wouldn't say that exactly.' Fier turned back to Grace leaving Kyle with the impression of dark unsmiling eyes above a smiling mouth. 'I'm sure I shall be able to think of something you can do for me one day!'

CHAPTER FOUR

THE sheer drop beneath the triple glazed floor-to-ceiling window running the full width of the room gave Kyle the impression she was still flying. She had woken up to the pale green haze and blowing daffodils of an English springtime morning, but spring was still weeks away from this eagle's nest in the Canadian Rocky Mountains. Snow still lay well beneath the tree line as well as on the mountain tops and there was ice on the glass outside. The sky was blue and nothing moved and she was alone in a vast white emptiness.

'You care for tea, ma'am?' She had spun round from the window, her heart hammering violently, before she realised that the voice belonged to someone else. Not to Fier but to the little man who had held the door of the helicopter open when she had arrived and whose face barely reached her shoulder.

'Yes—yes, please.' Still caught up in jet-lag, she stood uncertainly as he finished pushing the door he had so quietly opened back against the panelled wall and a maid appeared and walked past him with a heavy tray which she set down on a long, low table in front of the log fire.

'A hunter's tea.' Noticing her reaction to the apparently vast amount of food, the man grinned at her and winked. 'You'll get used to it!'

But she would never get used to it. She would never get used to the idea that someone, almost at a moment's notice, could transplant her from a world she had known all her life to one which was totally alien and strange.

Faucon d'Or—Golden Hawk—the luxury mountain retreat in the last of the wilderness. Fier Cailloux's wilderness.

'If there's anything else you want, just ring.' The little man nodded towards a bell rope beside the stone hearth. He was old and wizened—part Indian, too, Kyle guessed—and the slightly bandy legs in the denim jeans under the plaid work shirt looked as if they needed leather riding chaps to make them and their owner really comfortable.

'There is one thing.' She stopped him on his way out of the door. He was friendly, not like the other people she had so far met since the Boeing 747 had touched down at Edmonton. They had all been polite enough, but this man looked as if he sensed and genuinely cared about her feeling of being totally alone. 'Can you tell me when Mr Cailloux will be back, Mr ——?' She stopped awkwardly. She didn't know his name.

'Mace. Just Mace,' he supplied easily. 'And no, I cain't. Fier'll be back when he chooses—prob'ly before dark.'

'When he chooses!' The words repeated in Kyle's head as the man called Mace finished closing the door behind him and left her alone once more in the room with the huge window. They could be Fier Cailloux's motto; at least as far as the amount of control his inheritance had given him over her and Grace's lives.

She turned her back on the apparently never-ending range of mountains and walked across the deep pile carpet and poured herself some tea. There was no milk, just tea-bags in the silver pot, but it was good; delicate and faintly lemon flavoured. She stood in front of the blazing fire with both hands round the thin bone china cup.

Fier had chosen to leave them alone at Dovercourt all winter. Then, just when it seemed as if nothing was going to change, as if the life that he had interrupted was going to be allowed to resume its old, uneventful pattern, he had dropped his bombshell.

Ted Sully, fresh out of agricultural college with no more hope of farming in these inflation-ridden days than of one day taking over his father's tenant property, was to take over and manage the whole estate, and Kyle was to come to Canada.

At once, and just like that. On the basis of one transatlantic telephone call, and then not to her but to the estate's London solicitor, everything was to change.

It would never work, Kyle was sure of it. Old Frank Sully would never tolerate taking orders from his son about new-fangled ways of intensive farming, and as for wanting her to go to Canada . . .!

'You're sure it's me he wants?' she had said into the telephone.

'I hardly think I'm likely to have made a mistake about something as definite as that. Mr Cailloux was quite specific.' Over the telephone, another telephone, the solicitor's dry voice had been offended. 'A flight has been booked for you from London to Edmonton on Tuesday of next week—first class, of course,' he added as if that should be obvious. 'You will be met at Edmonton.' He was quoting from his notes. 'Arrangements are already in hand for a visa and your flight number, tickets and so forth are already in the post.'

The dry voice went on and on explaining, and as the library stopped spinning round her, the thought that she would be leaving Dovercourt for a long time—perhaps the last time—the following Tuesday became not a wild figment of her imagination but an already established fact.

But why her? Why had Fier asked for her? It was Grace he had admired, Grace who had gone away for Christmas and was still somewhere in Europe, skiing or *après*-skiing with an ever-changing group of friends. Kyle could still remember Fier's expression when he and Grace had said goodbye. He had paused above her upturned face and then gently, very gently, he had bent and kissed her cheek. Starting with their father bending over the net-draped cradle, it had been an expression and a gesture Kyle had been seeing all her life. The homage Grace demanded and received for her incredible golden beauty.

For her there had just been an ordinary goodbye. A glint, a gleam, perhaps, somewhere behind the surface of those cobalt eyes hinting at shared moments which could still make her skin burn when she remembered the controlled strength of fingers ripping the shoulder of her dress apart and then the sensual touch of those same fingers stroking the length of her bare throat in a seductive blackmail.

Had it really been almost a year since then? Had summer changed to winter and now to spring since the Mercedes had turned out of the drive at Dovercourt and taken Fier, as she had then thought, out of her life?

Once, just once, in the intervening months, she had heard of him—and then not heard, but read. A mention in the financial column of *The Times* about business interests she didn't know he had but which accounted for Grace's shrewd summation after he had left that he could more than afford the unkeep of both Dovercourt and his Canadian ranch. They had no need to feel guilty about staying on, Grace had shrugged. He could more than afford to pay for their keep.

But neither Kyle nor Grace—not even Grace—had heard from Fier in the months since his car had turned out of the drive. Looking back on it, the time seemed like both an eternity and a day, and now he wasn't back in her life; he had summoned her into his.

He needed a housekeeper for his guest ranch at Faucon d'Or: so went the message she had received at second hand. And where else should he look? she had asked herself more rationally when the first sense of disbelieving shock had gradually died away.

Grace *kept* servants; she wasn't one of them. Kyle remembered the constant arguments about the clothes-strewn battleground of Grace's room which she seemed to think was none of her responsibility to keep clean. It was Kyle who had shown herself capable of managing a big house and an estate. It was Kyle who was also the more likely to realise their moral obligation.

Fier's money hadn't just kept them through the winter. It was also paying, albeit without his knowledge, for the extended skiing holiday in Europe Grace was now enjoying. There had been a cheque enclosed with the airline ticket and the papers she had received, and she had written another cheque and sent it off to Grace's bank. The Haultain sisters had an obligation; Kyle acknowledged it, and Fier was calling in his debt. His astounding summons was no more—no less—than that, and as Grace was hardly the first person to spring to mind when it came to thinking in terms of a house-keeper, what could be more natural than that his thoughts should turn to the quiet one, the unobtrusive one—herself?

It was an intolerable situation, but he had left her no option but to accept.

The door behind her once more opened and Kyle once more spun round, heart thumping, breath catching in her throat. But it was the maid, come to clear away the tray.

'Is——' Kyle licked her lips, 'is Mr Cailloux back yet?'

'No, ma'am.' The girl nudged the door open with her elbow. 'You'll hear him when he comes.'

Should she go to her room or wait where she was? Kyle stood indecisive as the door quietly closed. And what did the girl mean, she would hear him when he came? Fier moved easily, quietly, like a cat. She could remember that. She blocked the other memories that tried to crowd her mind.

The room in which she was still standing appeared to be an office and something more. A long chesterfield and deep easy chairs were grouped around the heavy wooden coffee table in front of the log fire, but there was a desk in the far corner and filing cabinets. It was a man's room, somehow, private and, in front of the long window that both dominated and made it seem part of the never-ending space, there was another chair in which someone often sat. She could see the indentations of the body in the leather and whoever sat there would be gazing out over the range upon range of mountains like an eagle in its nest. Faucon d'Or—the golden hawk; but the hawk who brooded on this mountain top had cobalt eyes and jet black hair that had felt alive when her hands had brushed against it.

The chatter of helicopter blades—familiar now but totally strange until her arrival in Edmonton an hour or two earlier—came faintly through the triple glazing, and an ungainly shadow fluttered briefly over the nearest mountain top, pink now and turning gold in the light of the rapidly setting sun, as the machine dropped and veered out of her sight to land on the ranch's private helipad.

She knew she was an hour's flight away from Alberta's provincial capital of Edmonton. She also knew she was in the Rocky Mountains, miles north of Banff and Jasper, the two great national parks, and miles north again of the Willmore Wilderness Park, but apart from that, and the fact she was in Canada, she had no idea where she was. No wonder, when news of Fier's inheritance had first reached them all those months ago, she and Grace had spent so much wasted time poring over the old schoolroom atlas looking for a place called Faucon d'Or.

There was no way in or out in winter, the chopper pilot had informed her as they had flown through the high passes, except by air or on skis or snowshoes. Fier had been determined to keep his wilderness cut off and totally isolated.

A burst of noise surprised her; men's and women's voices talking excitedly, starting suddenly and just as suddenly cut off. She glanced across her shoulder and her heart missed a beat. The door had opened and closed silently behind him and Fier had come into the room.

'I see you're here.' His voice wasn't like the others. She had forgotten just how distinctively different it was with its underlay of French behind the clipped, hard syllables. 'Have you seen your room? Do you have everything you need?'

'Yes.' She started nervously, but then something

inside her snapped. No, dammit, she had not got everything she needed. She was entitled to some explanation, and she would demand it now before two dark pools of eyes could drill right through her skull, emptying it of all thoughts except unbidden ones. 'No,' she said, 'I haven't! I want to know what right you have to bring me here!'

He smiled, an alarming glint of white in his dark face and a moving shimmer beneath the cobalt surface of his eyes. Kyle thought she had forgotten, but she hadn't. He was familiar, too familiar, as he stood there watching her.

He must have been out skiing with the guests she had heard return, and the shoulders were just as broad, the stomach just as flat and the muscles in his legs and thighs were just as powerful as she now remembered in the second skin of his closely fitting ski clothes.

'None.' When it came, it was his answer that took her totally by surprise. 'No right at all.' He unzipped the short black jacket and threw it casually on a chair and the familiar lock of dark hair fell across his forehead. 'The right was yours,' he continued uncharacteristically mildly, 'to refuse.'

'When everything was cut and dried and decided for me, even down to the flight I had to take?' She just couldn't believe what he was saying. She had been presented with a *fait accompli*; an ultimatum; a take-it-or-leave-it choice, and she had chosen ... shock spiralled its way under the serviceable woollen dress. She had *chosen* to come! Where was the self-sufficiency about which she had boasted? She could type and keep books; she remembered telling him against a background of soft slow music at the supper club. If Dovercourt was sold, it would be Grace who would be most affected, she had explained. *She* would get a flat in London and a job. He hadn't sold Dovercourt, but, by appointing young Ted Sully as its manager, he had freed her of its responsibility and she had indeed taken a job ... this job! She turned her head; she couldn't let him go on watching her.

'I didn't realise I had a choice,' she mumbled awkwardly. But had she? Had she realised all along but blanked it out because this was the choice she wanted to make?

'I'm hardly a white slaver!' he said wryly. 'Whatever other opinion you may have of me, I'm hardly that! I made you a business offer which you accepted. I needed somebody here quickly and you came to mind.'

Suddenly, she had no doubt, when he was casting round to find a suitable replacement for the housekeeper who, for whatever reason, had inconveniently left. It was probably the first time he had thought of her since the Mercedes had turned out of the driveway whereas he had been in her mind far more frequently than she would acknowledge even to herself.

There were memories of him all over Dovercourt. In the farms, in the house, in the little half-timbered pub she passed occasionally. It was difficult not to be reminded of Fier Cailloux as she had gone about her daily routine.

'I misunderstood, then,' she said awkwardly. 'I'm sorry!'

Fier accepted her apology without comment. 'And now that's settled, we'd best put you to work!'

Kyle felt a flash of disappointment. It was to be just a job, after all.

'Have you seen over the house?' He hadn't appeared to notice.

'No.'

'We have no more than twelve guests here at any one time,' he continued smoothly, 'and we have thirty-nine staff. You will be in charge of the ones who work indoors. The keynote at Faucon d'Or is luxury and service. Our guests are paying guests and they pay heavily for the privilege of staying here.' Privilege, Kyle noted as he went on. He had opened the doors of his private wilderness, but only to the very few. 'We offer all the services of a five-star hotel in any major city in the world plus, depending on the time of year—skiing, trail riding, fishing and, if it's required, complete privacy.' He walked across and pulled the bell rope beside the fireplace. 'As my hostess as well as my housekeeper——' Kyle registered the addition to her role with a jolt, '—you will be expected to see that everyone staying here has the impression that they're staying in a private country home, and you have my complete authority to do everything necessary to achieve that goal. We dine at eight and,' Kyle saw his eyes narrow as he noticed the serviceable brown dress, 'we dress for dinner! And now,' the door behind him quietly opened, 'Mace will show you round.'

And that was it. He had hired her in an emergency; he had talked to her to confirm his judgment and he had now passed her over to a trusted member of his staff to ensure that she became acquainted with her duties. But then, as he had so rightly pointed out, he was hardly a white slaver. She could have refused his high-handed offer. She did, after all, have a mind—and will—of her own!

She had seen only the outside of the ranch, her room, two corridors, stairs and Fier's office since her arrival in the helicopter, and now she was amazed at how large it really was. Not on the same grand scale as Dovercourt, but built to fit into its wild environment with huge, milled redwood logs, dovetailed at the corners and chinked and filled to make them weatherproof.

Mace tapped one with his knuckle. 'Took the boss four years. Everything either flown in or packed in when the weather was good enough to get the horses up here!'

'Why did he do it?' Kyle frowned round the spacious entrance hall, used as a central lounge and empty now except for a whitecoated man emptying ashtrays and collecting glasses in the quiet hour as the guests changed for dinner.

'Dunno. Never asked,' Mace said shortly.

No, you wouldn't! You would never ask Fier his reasons for doing anything. You would wait until he told you—if he ever did. Kyle ran a hand over one of the logs, surprised at how warm it felt in spite of the biting cold outside. The cold, a different creature from the wet, cold English winters she had been used to, had been one of the things she had noticed when she had hurried inside from the helicopter, the other had been the outside of the ranch; a weathered silver-grey under its many-gabled, cedar-shingled roof. But inside, the logs had been treated with a substance that gave them a soft rich glow. It reflected the light from the many table lamps scattered around the lounge in which they were now standing and gave the impression of wilderness living mixed with total luxury.

There was an arched, ribbed ceiling of the same glowing wood, the carpet was heavy woollen pile and the floor-length curtains hid the gathering darkness outside the triple glazed picture windows.

'Ben, meet Mizz Haultain—Kyle—the new house-keeper.' Although he only came up to her shoulder, Mace seemed to have special rights. He was one of the staff and yet not one of them. Whatever her authority, it did not extend to Mace. No one had to tell her; she knew instinctively that he was Fier's man, answerable to him alone. As indeed she was, Kyle realised, as Mace completed the introductions.

'Isn't Marsha coming back, then?' The man called Ben, smooth in white jacket and black trousers, paused in his task of collecting cocktail glasses and looked her over curiously.

'Apparently she ain't,' Mace said shortly. 'Asks too many questions,' he added in an undertone. 'Now, where shall I take you? Some of the upstairs rooms is empty. You'd best see them.'

Stairways, corridors, a clinically immaculate kitchen under the control of a French chef; telex and radio for world-wide communication and an on-staff secretary. Under-cooks, under-housekeepers and maids; and guest suites more like staterooms on a liner each with its own luxury en-suite bath. An underground cistern for collecting water; stables flanking each wing of the house; a generator and a standby for power and two eight-seater Bell 206 helicopters. These were the facts and figures poured into her ears and eyes during Mace's introductory tour and, on top of them, faces— all strange faces, some welcoming, some openly curious like Ben, and the name of Marsha mentioned more than once, and each time killed abruptly by a close-lipped Mace.

Kyle supposed that one day—and one day not too far ahead, if she was to achieve the standard of smoothly efficient service the owner of all this unexpected luxury in the wilderness demanded from his staff—the names and faces and the geography of the rooms and corridors would be firmly established in her currently ringing head and she, too, would be catering to the needs of the handful of wealthy guests with the same assurance.

But for now, it was enough to throw off the serviceable woollen dress, take a quick shower in the bathroom leading from her more modest bedroom, and thank heaven she hadn't sent Fier's attempt to make her stand out from the wallpaper to the nearest jumble sale.

She consulted the thin gold wafer of her watch—a bridesmaid's gift from Grace and Alex—and fastened it back around her wrist. She had, she judged, ten minutes. Dinner was at eight, but a sixth sense told her that Fier would expect her down well before that to meet his guests.

She was—what had he said?—his hostess, not just his housekeeper, and when you started work for Fier Cailloux, the job obviously started from the moment you set foot from the helicopter on to the concrete helipad.

It would have been nice to have gone to bed early on her first night, but that wasn't Fier's way. A ten-hour, four or five-thousand-mile journey was irrelevant, and so were courtesies. There had been no questions about her first ever transatlantic flight; no enquiries about Thea or—more surprisingly—about Grace when he had walked into his eyrie of a den and found her waiting there. Just a quick, matter-of-fact summation of his reasons for summoning her there—a puncturing of her fantastical balloon—and then a handing over to another member of his staff for her first look at that part of his domain that was to be her responsibility.

The black silk of the dress she had worn just once slid seductively over her head. It was much too low. Her breasts strained at the daringly cut, boned bodice when she raised her arms to pile her soft, shoulder-length brown hair on top of her head and, suddenly, the woman she had seen only once before in her life was staring back at her from the dressing table mirror.

She regarded herself defiantly. It was the black dress or nothing. The cream silk taffeta had never recovered from Fier's attack and the money in Fier's cheque for incidental travelling expenses had gone to Grace, not to replenish her limited wardrobe. She applied lip-gloss and touched her tongue to her lips. What was making her so nervous? Dovercourt was safe—she trusted his word totally on that. For the time being, at least, she didn't have to worry; didn't have to think about Dovercourt with Ted Sully left in charge. And all she had been summoned for was a job. One that she was sure she could do.

Taking a deep breath, Kyle squared the naked shoulders rising from the lavish black foam of the ruffle and left the room.

'Good!' The word was there in Fier's quiet nod of approval when she walked into the almost empty lounge, but he was approving the intuition that had brought her down so early, not her looks, Kyle warned herself. Apart from the white-coated barman—Ben, Kyle frowned to remember—she and Fier were the only people there. A handsome couple waiting to greet their guests.

'If all else fails, you'll just have to marry him, that's all!' Why did Grace's frivolous comment have to pop into her head just then with Fier walking slowly in her direction? He had changed from the black ski clothes into a beautifully cut black dinner suit and bow tie, and the snowy brilliance of his linen accentuated the striking darkness of his face. He was smiling and the light danced in his cobalt eyes.

'What will you have to drink?'

'Plain ginger ale.' The last thing she wanted was to get tipsy, particularly as the hand laid gently on her elbow was already doing alarming things to her metabolism.

There was another nod of quiet approval as Ben materialised at her elbow with a half full champagne glass of golden fizzing liquid on a silver tray. Then footsteps sounded on the stairs behind them, the hand underneath her elbow tightened and the evening had begun.

'Ah, Sir Geoffrey!' Fier turned her smoothly towards the white haired man reaching the last stair. 'No serious after-effects from your tumble? Ben, a Chivas for Sir Geoffrey, and while we're waiting, may I introduce Kyle Haultain?'

Total privacy, first-class skiing for novices and experts alike and a mountain wilderness experience available in few other places in the world, had drawn an exclusive group to Faucon d'Or. Two millionaires with wives, a Canadian power broker who, if rumours were correct, controlled markets running into billions and an English rock star, the rumours of whose presence would have been enough to bring fans scrambling even to this remote mountain top, sat around the candlelit dinner table an hour later. Fier was at the head with Kyle facing him across silver candlesticks and a low, specially flown in, centrepiece of out-of-season flowers.

Kyle had recognised one of them. Sir Geoffrey Stevens, millionaire armaments manufacturer and racehorse owner with a wife whose outrageous Ascot hats claimed the headlines every year. The others had been unknown to her, especially the rock star. She had seen his face hundreds of times, of course, and heard his music blaring out but the tall, serious-countenanced young man with glasses and a companion who not only appeared to be considerably older but had no resemblance to the glossy women with whom his name was always linked, had been a total stranger.

'Don't worry,' he had muttered for her ears only when Fier had introduced them and he had noticed her surprise, 'no one knows me when I'm like this!' His eyes had grinned. 'This is what I *really* look like, and my real name's Stanley!'

Nine people and a staff of thirty-nine to cater to them. No, seven. She and Fier were also staff—at least—Kyle shrugged mentally, she was. Her head spun from the effort of remembering names and fighting off the tiredness that came from a thirty-one hour day. She glanced covertly at her watch. Just past nine o'clock, but four in the morning at Dovercourt where she had woken up.

The meal had been cooked and presented to Tour d'Argent standards and the service had flowed like oiled silk. Someone—Fier, she suspected—had also extended his long day to fill the gap left by her predecessor's abrupt departure. What was her name? Kyle's forehead wrinkled. Marsha!

'It's the image people build of you in their minds that counts.' The rock star on her left was talking.

'Give them a preconceived idea of what you are and what you look like and they won't look any further.' Was it her imagination or did Fier, apparently deep in conversation with Nora Stevens, glance up at her? 'Take me, for instance. I could go into any pub or store and they wouldn't have a clue. But give them a touch of the old Cockney, take off the windows and lay it on heavy, man!' He took off his hornrims and changed his voice to Nashville-London. 'And you've got a riot! God!' He leaned back in his chair and replaced his glasses. 'And to think I went to the Guildhall School of Music!'

'Darling, what time is it?' His wife—mistress?— touched his arm.

'Four days to going back to it all,' he replied laconically. 'I don't know, Syb, why ask me?'

'It's just after nine,' Kyle volunteered.

'Then it's past three in England, isn't it?' The quietly attractive face looked anxious. 'Come on, Stan, let's go on up. They're patching a call through home in a few hours' time. I promised I'd speak to the children every morning before they went to school,' she explained generally.

'Sorry, darlin'!' The face that graced millions of album covers rose inches away from Kyle's. 'You've gotta keep some of the illusions of a mad, bad rock star. A wife and two small kids just doesn't match the image! Goodnight, Miss Haultain,' he was himself, smiling down at her. 'See you, Fier. Lady Stevens, Mrs Ridgeley, gentlemen!'

'Skiing tomorrow, Stan!' Fier's distinctive voice floated down the table.

'You can bet on it!' the singer replied enthusiastically.

Their departure broke up the group around the dinner table, but there was coffee and brandy in the lounge; the brandy served by Ben and the coffee by Kyle, sitting behind the silver tray fighting the lead weights that threatened to close her eyes.

'I don't think we've been introduced.' The heavy-set man who had come down later than all the others but who had watched her almost continuously throughout dinner, eyes sliding across her bare neck and shoulders, was now in front of her. He had been standing with one of the other groups in the firelit lounge, deferred to even by the other two influential men by reason of his enormous financial influence in the world, but now he was in front of her.

'Merle Hubbard,' he introduced himself.

'Kyle Haultain.' She took the extended hand and forced her eyes up along the dinner-jacketed arm to the watchful, fleshy face. The head was over-large, set squarely on thick shoulders without apparent benefit of a neck, but there was no mistaking the power that hung about him.

'May I?' He indicated the space on the chesterfield beside her.

'Oh, yes, please do.' She moved slightly to give him room, but even so, he managed to brush against her as he sat.

'You're new here, I believe, Miss Haultain—it is *Miss* Haultain, isn't it?' Obsidian eyes that took in everything, but gave nothing of their owner's thoughts away, glanced down at her ringless fingers.

'Yes, it is.' His interest made her feel uncomfortable. 'And yes, I am new here. I arrived this afternoon.' She spoke over-brightly to compensate and, across the room a dark head lifted and Fier glanced across at them.

'From England?'

'Yes.' She tried to focus her attention on her companion, but the way he watched her sent a shiver down her spine. Eating her up was the only expression her tired mind could think of. Why didn't someone come and rescue her? But Fier had turned away—and then why should anyone come and rescue her? It was her job to be pleasant to the guests. Fier was doubtless feeling satisfied. 'A long way to come just for a job,' Hubbard remarked without emphasis. 'Was there any special reason?'

Yes! Because she had no choice—or thought she hadn't until Fier had so bluntly disabused her. But that was hardly something she could say. 'Fier—Mr Cailloux—suggested it,' she answered evasively, 'and it seemed a good opportunity to see Canada.'

'Then you haven't been here before?'

'No—no, I haven't.' Why wouldn't he look away?

'There's a lot to see,' he said blandly, 'and it's not all in the West. Here,' a gold fountain pen and a square plain card materialised, 'let me give you my private number and invite you to Toronto.'

'It's very kind of you, but I don't think . . .!'

'Another brandy, sir?' If looks could kill, Ben would have been stone dead. The barman arrived behind Merle Hubbard's shoulder just as the card was being pressed into her hand and, behind Ben, Fier, across the room, a look of tightly drawn displeasure on his face.

'Not now!' Hubbard snapped it out, but the interruption brought another guest across with an empty brandy glass and Kyle laid the card beside the coffee tray. The incident had distracted Hubbard's attention, that was all that mattered, but she was tired, so tired, when Sir Geoffrey Stevens finally levered himself from his chair beside the fire and loudly announced his intention of calling it a day.

'What time's the chopper leaving, Cailloux?' he asked heavily.

'Around ten.' If Fier felt any resentment about being treated as a lesser being, he showed no sign of it. Kyle wondered why he opened Faucon d'Or to visitors. He wasn't in the same class as Merle Hubbard—even Kyle had heard the name of the enormously powerful Bay Street billionaire when she stopped to think of it—but Fier had investments, holdings, a brain that was financially sharp enough to win him recognition in the financial columns.

Why then, when he obviously had no financial reason, did he not only make Faucon d'Or accessible to visitors but run the risk of self-important boors like Geoffrey Stevens? The dark face above the immaculate white linen gave no hint of any answer as the British armaments manufacturer went portentously on.

'Then have the masseur expect me around nine,' he said. 'I may have left it late in life to learn to ski, but I'm damned if I'm going to let one fall stop me!'

Goodnight, goodnight, goodnight; the remaining guests at last filed up the stairs and Kyle stood uncertainly. She should, she supposed, stay on. Fier was deep in conversation now with Ben, and although she would not be able to contribute, she supposed she should at least stay on and listen to a discussion about the finer points of wine cellar management. It would be a start to her education about the backstage work necessary to ensure a front of such effortless luxury. But she was tired—so tired.

'Goodnight.' Neither Fier nor Ben appeared to hear her and she walked quietly up the stairs, her dress catching on the thick pile of the carpet and baring one long leg as the slit skirt fell away. She might have been too tired to contribute much to the general conversation, but at least her appearance hadn't let Fier down. She caught hold of the dragging skirt and held it above her ankles and the stairs went more easily. What was it Stan Reynolds had been saying over dinner? Image was everything?—something like that. Fier had said the same thing once before, albeit much more forcibly. But even Fier must have been satisfied with her tonight. Merle Hubbard had more than confirmed that. When was the last time a Canadian billionaire had been unable to keep his eyes from her for more than five consecutive seconds?

The top stair arrived at last and she automatically turned right. The long corridor stretched ahead, glowing with polished wood and the reds, blacks and browns of the striking series of Cree and Haida paintings that lined the walls. Her room was at the end, and finally she reached the door and opened it.

Strange—she was sure she had left the bedside light on when she went downstairs, but someone had obviously been in and switched it off. She flicked the switch and the empty room sprang into life. But it wasn't hers. She should have turned left, not right, at the top of the stairs. She remembered now. This was one of the empty guest suites Mace had shown her on their tour that afternoon. Her room was down the *other* end.

Kyle switched off the light and retraced her steps along the thickly carpeted corridor. The lounge below was dark now, she noticed as she went past. Fier and Ben had finished their conversation about the cellar and disappeared. The other end of the corridor lay ahead: five more minutes and she would be in bed. She slipped off her shoes and held them in her hand and her quiet progress became noiseless. Stan and Sybil Reynolds, at least, would certainly be sleeping.

She reached the end of the corridor, but instead of a door, the well of a far less impressive flight of stairs leading to the kitchens and back offices opened up beside her. She was *still* wrong! She stood still and forced herself to concentrate, trying to visualise a floor plan of the building in her head. There were two floors but lots of corridors. She must have missed a turning further back. She began to walk back again, jet-lag and fatigue combining to make her feel curiously disorientated and at a loss. It was ridiculous, but she had no idea where she was. She doubted if she could even find the lounge. Her breath began to catch in long ragged gasps and she felt panicky. She had to find her room—she had to! She couldn't go on walking up and down long corridors all night carrying her shoes.

She turned through a previously unseen alcove and saw a door. Surely this must be it! She turned the handle and a sleepy voice grunted as a shaft of light fell across the bed.

'Get out of there!' The door was gently closed, but not before her fingers had been wrenched from the handle. 'What the hell do you think you're doing?' Fier demanded on a long, furious breath.

'I couldn't find my room.' His anger was not only visible but tangible as she turned to face him; touching her naked shoulders and draining all the colour from her face.

'Which accounts for the fact of no negligee, I suppose?' he said icily. 'However,' he glanced down, 'I see you've at least saved him the trouble of taking off your shoes!'

What had she done? Why was he so angry? Nothing made any sense as her arm was gripped with a force that made her wince and she found herself being propelled around another corner towards another door. He leaned past her and opened it and half threw her inside. It slammed and when she found her feet, he was standing with his back against it.

'Right,' he said, 'now you can explain!'

The feminine clutter on the dressing table was familiar and so was the nightdress she had laid out on the bed earlier. She had found her room at last. Everything was familiar except the man blocking the only exit with his shoulders.

It was Fier, but it could have been a total stranger. His nose was pinched and arrogant with the effort of control. His eyes were black in a suddenly paler face and the cords stood out against the dull sheen of his throat. The dinner jacket had disappeared and so had the tie, and she could see the dark movement of his chest through the tightly stretched silk shirt. He was breathing heavily and, as they stood, his breaths became a counterpoint to the sudden rapid beating of her heart.

'What were you doing going into Hubbard's room?'

'Nothing!' A part of her mind still registered that it was Hubbard and not Haggard and made a mental note, but her voice was strange and jerky. He was making her feel guilty. 'I couldn't find my room—it was a mistake!'

'I'm sure it was,' he said sarcastically, 'except that I was the mistake. I wasn't supposed to be wandering around the house making a last check. I was supposed to be in bed, like all the rest. When did you arrange it, Kyle? Was it over dinner? A few looks and a silent understanding. Or was it later when you were talking in the lounge? I must say, I give you credit for discretion—no one would have guessed! Merle Hubbard—my God! Is that what it takes to turn you on? Power?'

The anger that had been incomprehensible until that moment was illuminated by a great atomic flash. The man in the bed; the sleepy grunt when light from the half open door had fallen across his face; she had been going into Merle Hubbard's room and Fier thought—she blazed at the realisation of what Fier thought.

'I had no idea whose room it was,' she retorted furiously. 'I thought it was mine! I was tired and I was lost!'

'Please!' He said it wearily. 'Spare me the lies. You're trying to tell me you were lost on the bedroom floor of a two-storey house that's built in a square. A house you were shown around this afternoon—and in some considerable detail, if I know Mace!' She tried to speak, but his hand went up and she fell silent. Part French, part English and part Indian: it was all Indian facing her now with no common basis for communication. 'And as for being tired—if you were so tired,' he said insultingly, 'why were you still wandering around a good ten minutes after you slunk away from the lounge?'

She had not just been tired, she had been adrift; totally at a loss, but even to her, it sounded feeble as she saw the situation through his eyes.

Thrown into the company of one of the most powerful men in Canada—a man whose interest had been obvious from the moment he had walked into the dining room and seen her sitting there—what could be more natural than that a response had been aroused and that inhibitions that had applied in England had crumbled here. But Merle Hubbard? She remembered the squat body and the speculative assessment in those sliding eyes and was repelled.

'I run a hotel here, not a bawdy house!' Fier used a cruder word. 'We indulge our guests, but not to that extent. If you found it hard to sleep, you should have come to me—I could have made it easy for you!'

He didn't run for seven days, he ran for seven nights as well! His sibilant whisper, the way he moved towards her in one long stride, stirred a sudden recollection of a much earlier determination. 'Tell me, Kyle,' the eyes were blue now as he stepped into the circle of light thrown by the bedside lamp; blue but glittering under the errant lock of jet black hair, 'was he expecting you, or was your discreet arrival planned as a surprise? Was he going to do this . . . and this . . .?' He caught her hand and pulled her arm straight down against her side. The shoes she held went clattering to the floor. and her breasts rose above the low cut bodice of her dress, straining against the extravagant black ruffle.

'Fier, stop!' The silk felt harsh against her barely covered nipples and her throat went hollow as his eyes passed over it to linger on the swelling curves beneath.

She raised her free arm instinctively, but, instead of stopping her, his hand slipped round her waist, fingers reaching confidently for the tiny metal tag and the zip that held her bodice opened smoothly down her naked back.

'No!' Her gasp was killed as his lips found the pulse spot beating in her throat and then went on to leave a trail of fire burning on her arched neck until they reached their final resting place.

Somehow he was carrying her. And somehow, far from fighting him, her hands were round his neck, reliving memories of touching the vibrant darkness of his hair, and his teeth and lips were tasting hers as they plucked and nibbled the soft inner flesh of her yielding mouth.

The sudden surge of sensuality was overwhelming and her hand slid down inside his shirt; silk against the back of it and strong hard flesh with the heartbeat thudding underneath her palm. She felt the muscles tense as he lowered her and as the softness of the bed came up to take her, the weights that held her eyelids closed released their hold and she looked up from her tumbled nest of black silk and white pillows to find him standing over her. Against the light, every ligament and muscle in his body was hard and taut; an image in black and white with two hard pools of cobalt blue studying the wanton pattern of inky silk lapping rose and white as she lay on the bed in front of him. The fingers that had earlier gripped her wrist were now half hidden in the ruffles of his shirt and the dark skin of his chest gleamed dully to his waist as the tiny buttons were slowly wrenched undone.

Her whole being reached towards him, but it was the eyes that made her suddenly sit up, clutching the supple folds of silk around her. Those eyes held victory—and they held contempt.

'What is it, Kyle?' He saw her change of mood. 'Am I a couple of million short of your intentions?'

He almost seemed satisfied; as if her resistance had proved a point. What could she say? That the sudden realisation of her need had left her horrified? That he was totally wrong about Merle Hubbard? That, after this, no man—whether millionaire or pauper—could

Harlequin reaches
into the hearts and minds
of women across America
to bring you

Harlequin American Romance.™

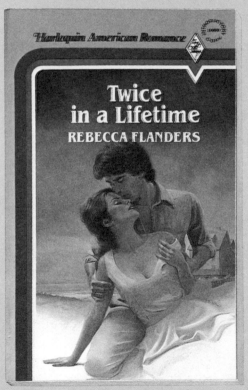

TWICE IN A LIFETIME

Rebecca Flanders

CHAPTER ONE

BARBARA sat in the crowded airport lounge, waiting for her flight to be called, and fingered the letter of invitation from her sister somewhat uncertainly. Barbara was twenty-six years old, self-sufficient, and mature, and she had been managing her own life since the first day she had left home for the independence of the state university. But, sitting alone amid the bustle and confusion of excited travelers, she felt somewhat like a lost and frightened child. She had felt that way a lot since Daniel had died.

She had been widowed a little over a year, and she knew her sister, via long-distance conferences with their mother, was worried about her. Perhaps with good cause, Barbara had to admit uneasily, for although most of the time Barbara managed to convince herself she was getting along just fine, there were still feelings of bitterness and periods of black depression she did not seem to be able to control. Of course it was a tragedy to be widowed so young, and everyone commiserated, everyone claimed to understand what she was going through. The real tragedy was that no one understood. No one could understand what it was to lose the one and only love of her life, not just a husband, but a lover and a friend... Most people would go their entire lives without ever finding what she and Daniel had shared, and to have their life together severed so abruptly and so cruelly was more than unfair, it was incomprehensible...

But Barbara wasn't meant to be alone for long. Follow her as she rediscovers the beauty of love. Read the rest of "Twice in a Lifetime" **FREE**.

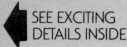

possibly mean what he now meant to her? But she had
said that once, and he had not believed her. She
watched the fingers refastening the small pearl buttons
and her body ached. She wanted him, but not like this;
not as a victory.

'I can't . . . I don't . . .!' Her mind refused to let her
find the words.

'Isn't it a bit late for that?' The cutting edge of his
voice tore into her. 'What are you? Twenty-seven—
twenty-eight? I almost believed, you know,' the voice
turned conversational, 'I almost believed that you were
what you made out to be!'

A repressed spinster of the species; outshone by
Grace and Thea. A virgin with no affairs—no loving—
hidden in her past. He had no need to go on.

'However, as we have now found the truth,' the shirt
was buttoned now and he paused on the point of leaving her, 'perhaps I should remind you what your duties
are. You are here to run my home and give my guests
the impression that they are staying in a private
country house and, as far as the guests are concerned,
especially the male ones, your services———' he turned
it into a substitute for a much more unpleasant word,
'—stop short at that. Hubbard will be leaving in ten
days. Between now and then you will have absolutely
nothing more to do with him than is absolutely unavoidable!'

Come back! You don't understand! The cry echoed
in her head, but what was the use of calling after him?
Kyle held herself rigidly erect against the pillows as he
turned away and walked across the room, and her love
went through the door.

CHAPTER FIVE

BEN, Charlene, Mace, Crystal, Lucy—Kyle repeated and re-repeated the names of the indoor staff in an effort to remember them. *She couldn't possibly be in love.* Ben was the barman-cum-butler who also waited at table as well as supervising the cellar. In a restaurant of the standard of Faucon d'Or, he would probably be called the *sommelier*. Charlene, a pretty girl with long dark hair tied smoothly back, also waited on tables and took care of the dining room and lounge. Mace—Mace of the wizened face and bandy legs was one apart. He was Fier's man—responsible to Fier alone. But Crystal and Lucy were two more of the indoor maids; she could hear one of them now, busy with a vacuum cleaner.

And if she was in love, when could it possibly have happened?

There were more staff she hadn't met, having time off in Edmonton. Another one of her responsibilities; making sure the staff came and went in one or other of the helicopters without the slightest disruption to the guests. There was a flow chart thumb-tacked to the wall of the tiny office she had been allocated behind the kitchen and she could see herself reflected in its shiny plastic surface, her lips moving as she repeated all the names in an effort of rote learning while thoughts in another, much more private memory bank ran underneath the surface of her mind.

Had it been over lunch in the pub, perhaps, when she scarcely knew him? Or had it been that night with Grace and Thea when dancing with his arms around her had been like dancing in a dream until, that was, he had pricked the bubble of her dangerous fantasy by switching the conversation back to Grace.

But she mustn't think of Fier. She had to concentrate. Kyle drowned at her dim reflection in the plastic flow chart. The first step of getting this new job under her control was getting well acquainted with her staff. She had been used to two—Manuel and Fernanda, left behind at Dovercourt as caretakers—she now had almost twenty. Perhaps if she tried repeating their names alphabetically, she could fix them more easily in her head. Ben, Charlene, Crystal, Lucy—a name and a fleeting mental picture of what each looked like and what they did, all overridden by a much clearer picture of another face hard and mocking with contempt.

Until now—eight almost sleepless hours after he had abruptly left her—she hadn't realised how clearly she had remembered or how often dwelt upon her first experience of being in Fier's arms that night when they were dancing. It had seemed so right—so natural. A place where she belonged.

No—she wouldn't think like that.

She tried the names of the staff again, reaching into her memory for more, but it was useless, just as loving Fier was useless. When or where it started was immaterial. What counted was that loving him was self-inflicted grief.

What a fool she was! She had gone through life not caring, scarcely even noticing, the rare occasions when a man had shown her any special interest. Like the Sleeping Beauty, albeit unconsciously, she had been waiting. But whereas the Sleeping Beauty had been awakened with a kiss, her love had been aroused by a man whose strongest feeling for her was contempt.

A quiet knock made her heart stop beating, but it was Mace's aged yet ageless face that appeared when the door opened. He was holding a sheaf of papers covered with sprawling writing.

' 'Iplite——' the closest the old wrangler ever came to Hippolyte, the French chef's name, Kyle was to discover, '—'Iplite sent these for you to do the orderin'. They're the menus for next week.'

Kyle took the sheets of closely written papers and started to study them. Her first day's work at Faucon d'Or was now fully under way.

The twenty or so staff under her control pulled smoothly: the others she rarely saw. The pilot and the ski-instructor; the staff in the fully equipped gymnasium and spa, all these and more came under Fier's control, and Fier, too, was also a near stranger.

She had the worst of both worlds, she decided. Seeing him constantly but never coming close. Facing him across the long, candlelit dinner table but talking only to the guests and then, later, over coffee and liqueurs, aware of a disturbing presence on the edge of her line of sight, sometimes watching her but more often not.

It was only during the day that she had peace of mind.

Then Fier and the young pilot who had brought her from Edmonton flew guests to otherwise inaccessible mountain tops to ski on slopes that had never before had man leave his mark on their crisp surfaces and while they were away, she could immerse herself in work. Inspecting guest suites after the maids had cleaned, checking and re-checking on the details that made the difference between service and total luxury until, at the end of the first week, it seemed as if she had never in her life done anything except ensure that Faucon d'Or was run to Fier's exacting standards.

Skills she hadn't consciously known she possessed came to her aid as she put what she had learned through the years of running Dovercourt into practice in her new life. She should feel satisfied. She was a person of some importance; a being in her own right. Totally complete, except when she relaxed her mental discipline and found herself thinking of the might-have-been with Fier.

The cab that dropped her at the corner of One-Ten and Jasper disappeared into the mêlée of traffic negotiating its way around the latest barrier thrown up to mark the progress of the newest phase of Edmonton's underground transit system. It was less cold here. The province of Alberta's busy capital was a hundred or so miles south of Faucon d'Or and several thousand feet nearer sea level, but the wind coming whipping round the corner had grit from the excavations in its teeth. It cut through the winter coat she had brought from England and she had trouble holding the street map steady in her hand.

'You looking for somewhere?' A man had stopped, his face red with cold under the fur flaps of his hat.

'Yes—here.' She pointed. Would anyone have stopped in London in this weather? She doubted it.

But her knight in the quilted armour of his sheepskin coat seemed impervious to the sub-sub-zero temperature. 'Turn left down there,' he told her, 'and two blocks north. You can't miss it.'

If anyone had also told her just three weeks earlier

that, on this late March day, she would be walking along the snow-banked sidewalks of a totally strange city on her way to a wholesale food importers, Kyle would have said they were being ridiculous. If anyone had told her just three weeks earlier that she would now know the agony of being hopelessly in love, she would have said they were mad.

She found the grey-fronted building she had been looking for and pushed her way into an aromatic world. Victuallers and International Food Importers, said the sign above the door; an outfitter's outfitter! She winced at the irony. The company had probably started just about the same time as Fier's ancestors were guiding the first groups of curious English aristocracy through the Rockies or packing food on strings of horses to the gold prospectors and rail construction crews.

'Marsha! Good to see you!' The man behind the desk in the small partitioned office into which the receptionist ushered her spoke before he saw her clearly, but then his broad smile wavered. 'I'm sorry!' He got up and came around the desk towards her, hand outstretched. 'I was expecting Marsha Vincey.' And he was disappointed.

'I've taken over from her.' Marsha Vincey! The ghost at her shoulder. This was by no means the first time her name had been mentioned. A slip of the tongue, hastily covered over, or just its unconscious use, but just about everyone with whom she had come into contact over the past week had forgotten and called her Marsha. Everyone, that was, with one exception. For Fier, Marsha Vincey might never have existed.

'As housekeeper at Faucon d'Or? Yes, yes, of course!' The mixed emotions on the face inspecting her smoothed into another smile. 'Sit down,' the eyes flicked to her ringless fingers, 'sit down, Miss . . .?'

'Haultain—Kyle Haultain.'

'When did Marsha—Miss Vincey—quit?' The question came with studied casualness at the end of almost an hour's discussion about prices and quantities as Kyle filled the list she had brought with her from the ranch. Not quite caviar and quails' eggs, but almost. There was certainly caviar—Beluga, if possible, but there was also flour for Hippolyte's delicious crusty French bread and other, more down-to-earth commodities, such as soap and cleaning fluid. It was Kyle's responsibility to see that freezers and storage cupboards never ran short of anything, no matter how exotic or mundane, and it was the boast of this particular firm of importers that they could supply it. Hence her first trip away from Faucon d'Or since she had arrived.

'I think Miss Vincey left about two weeks ago.' Kyle ticked the last empty space on her list beside Floris soap and started to gather her things together.

'It's odd she didn't say anything.'

Kyle glanced up, enquiring. There was a photograph on the desk—a woman and two small children.

'Marsha was here about two weeks ago—we usually had lunch. She didn't say anything about leaving then.' The man frowned.

'Perhaps she was called away suddenly—family business, that sort of thing?' Kyle offered.

'Yeah, yeah, that was probably it.' He brightened. 'Say,' he went on confidentially, 'you wouldn't happen to have a forwarding address for her, would you?'

No, she hadn't. She also had neither the time nor the inclination to accept an over-pressing invitation to her for lunch. The days were getting longer now at the end of March, but she still had only an hour or two before she would have to get a cab back to the airport and meet Mike with the helicopter so that they could make the flight to Faucon d'Or before the last of the light had gone, and she had no intention of spending that hour or two as Marsha Vincey's substitute.

She left the building in a state of slight resentment. There had obviously been more changes than the one that had brought her four thousand-odd miles from home and left her dealing confidently with a morning's business that had involved spending considerable amounts of someone else's money: she had changed inside herself. She had spent her life in Grace and Thea's shadow, but now, after only a week at Faucon d'Or, she was no longer prepared to be a substitute for anyone—far less the unknown Marsha Vincey.

She let herself build on her unusual sense of grievance. She was Kyle Haultain, a person of some importance. Rock stars and millionaires found her interesting—one had even found her too intriguing!

Along with Stan and Sybil Reynolds, Merle Hubbard had flown out from Faucon d'Or the day before. There was power and there was power, Kyle had found herself reflecting as, her duties as hostess done, she had stood beside the helipad and watched Fier make his goodbyes. Nothing had been said, she was sure of that, and the enormously influential Canadian billionaire was hardly likely to have remembered his bedroom door being opened that first night, far less know whose hand had opened it. He certainly couldn't know—standing there in the biting cold, Kyle flushed at the memory—about the scene that had taken place immediately afterwards, and yet something had warned him to stay away from her and the eyes that had once appreciatively assessed her, now looked elsewhere. A message had been sent. Power had given way to power—Fier's brand of power. The sort that could, at the nod of a dark head, send a helicopter lifting off to take Merle Hubbard and the Reynoldses skimming off over the mountain tops on the first stage of their journey out of his wilderness.

Fier had turned as the helicopter had gained height and, catching sight of her, his mouth had narrowed into its familiar, hard straight line. He was satisfied. Temptation had taken off into the skies. There was no need for him to watch her now.

Standing in the snow-bound streets of Edmonton a day later, Kyle pushed the humiliating memory of that smile into the background of her mind. She had two hours before she was due back at the airport to meet Mike and the staff returning from their days off and fly back with them and two new guests to Faucon d'Or. Rather than dwell on Fier's doubtless still unflattering opinion of her, she would better to use the time in hand to buy herself some clothes. What she had were hardly suitable for the role of hostess at an exclusive mountain hideaway; always excepting the black dress, of course, and that seemed to have trouble stitched into every seam.

She found the Bay and turned gratefully out of the cold March weather into the heated interior of the busy department store. There was a metal plaque on the wall outside, tracing the history of the site from Hudson Bay frontier fort and trading post to what it was today in little more than a hundred years. Passing it, Kyle felt a sense of fellow feeling. The course of her life, too, had undergone radical and sweeping changes in an incredibly short time.

*

'This was in the mail Mike picked up in Edmonton. It's for you.' New guests settled in, the staff who had flown back with her taking over from those who had since left for their time off in the city as smoothly as if they had never been away and now Fier—standing in the doorway of her tiny office with a letter in his hand.

Kyle's nerves began to hum like high-tension wires. 'Thank you.' She had no need to look up to know that he had walked across to her. She took the letter cautiously; careful to keep her fingers the width of the blue airmail envelope away from his.

'I'm sorry!' Now she looked up—straight into the face that was looking down at her; the penetrating cobalt of the eyes heightened and intensified by the dark, high-necked ski sweater and the unruly darkness of the hair. She didn't know he knew *how* to apologise! 'I'm sorry!' He confirmed he did. 'I opened it with the rest before I realised it was for you. It's from your sister.'

So Grace *did* know she was in Canada—and had opening the letter really been a mistake? The two thoughts overlapped each other in Kyle's head. The Countess Grace Orsinski—Grace might have left the man, but the title carried too much clout for her to give it up—and the name and return address were clear enough in the splashy writing on the envelope. Could she really blame Fier if he had succumbed to the temptation of finding out more about the irresistible Haultain sister and had opened it? It was as unlikely as the apology—but it was possible.

'It doesn't matter,' she said, and waited for him to leave. Instead he stood there, apparently absorbed in the information on the plastic flow chart on the wall in front of him. 'Excuse me!' She opened the envelope and slid the single sheet of folded paper out. She couldn't just go on sitting there.

'Sure.' He glanced at her and glanced away.

'Darling,' Grace had written, 'Alex is being difficult again, threatening to cut off my allowance unless I go back to him—can you imagine? I might, I suppose, one day, but *not*——' the word was heavily underlined, '—while he's being so absolutely beastly! What do you think? Should I—or shouldn't I? Anyway, do you think you could ask Fier if he could send me something? Not much—just a little something once a month. I think I'm entitled, after all, with him getting everything! Anyway, Kylie, do see what you can do! Oh, and PS—lots of love!'

And that was it. A little more in a second postscript about where to find her and what her plans were for the next few weeks, but nothing about Kyle or about the incredible alteration that had taken place in *her* life. In typically Grace fashion, unless what was happening was happening to her, it was of no interest. That's what came of being the centre of attraction all your life, Kyle thought ruefully. Of knowing that, without any effort on your part, you would never be short of love. She felt suddenly and indescribably depressed.

'Is it bad news?' The man who was in part responsible for that feeling of hopelessness made her look up in surprise. She had actually forgotten he was there! Forgotten that she had only to reach out a hand to touch the strength of that hard body.

'No, not bad news.' She schooled her face to hide a sudden longing while her mind worked furiously. Should she, or should she not, tell him about Grace's demand for money? No. There were already enough obligations. She would find the money from her salary and send it to Grace herself. 'I was just surprised, that's all,' she went on quietly. 'Grace says she might go back to Alex.'

'I see.' He went absolutely still. 'And does she say when the great reconciliation is going to take place?'

'No!' Just as she hadn't exactly said that she was thinking of going back to Alex. Kyle stepped round the small distortion. 'She's still considering.'

He snorted, half amused. 'And the man in question has no say? How like your sister! Tell me,' he asked intently, 'what do you think? Do you think she should go back?'

The irony of the situation struck her. 'If she loves him, yes. But how can you tell anyone who they're to love?' Certainly no one had ever told her to fall in love with Fier.

'One of the world's great truths,' he agreed laconically, 'and I daresay in the end, she'll make up her own mind. Let me know how it progresses.' Why was he so concerned? Kyle wondered. But then every man she met, however briefly, had some concern for Grace, and it had been that way ever since she had been born.

'Incidentally,' Fier stopped on his way to the door with a knowing smile carving lines on his lean face, 'is Grace asking you for money?'

'No.' She was being perfectly honest, Kyle rationalised. Grace hadn't asked her for a penny; she had asked her to ask Fier. But there was no need to tell him that, or that she intended to try and help Grace out herself.

'Really?' He was clearly sceptical. 'I'm surprised.

However, if—and when—she does, I suggest you refuse.'

'And let her starve, I suppose?' Kyle said sarcastically.

'I hardly think she'll do that,' he countered wryly. 'I do, however, think that she should learn to stand on her own two feet!'

The door clicked shut and the tension that had filled it left the room. He was shrewder about Grace than she had thought, Kyle realised, but that was probably because Grace wasn't there. One look at her and he would melt, like all the rest. With Fier Cailloux, the process would just take a little longer than with most other men.

It was just possible to go on working there—and now she really had no choice, with money from her handsome salary going to Grace each month—but sometimes, when an unguarded moment found her watching Fier with all the anguish of a sense of loss for something she had never had, she wondered how long she could continue. A few moments in his arms, and then not lovingly but as an angry demonstration of his anger and contempt. A lesson taught—and learned—and never once referred to; that had been all she had had, but it had shown her what the impossible could be like.

And along with loving came waves of fierce, resentful anger of her own. Why hadn't he let her be? Why had he summoned her from England and moulded the new image that had been responsible for that catalytic scene? She had been happy at Dovercourt, or at least, if not totally happy with her life, she had been content. There were definite advantages in fading into the background with the wallpaper, no matter what Fier might think.

Her visa gave her six months in Canada, and in the first three of those months, first spring and then early summer came to Fier's mountain top. Kyle could see the seasons change beneath them, moving gradually up the slopes. First the faint green in the valley and then a deeper solid green as grass and short scrub willow threw out new fresh growth. The birds came back—golden eagles soaring and whiskey jacks flirting in the branches above roaring streams swollen with melting snow. Only peaks higher than Faucon d'Or stayed white under their permanently frozen caps, and, as the snow receded, so life changed at the ranch.

The helicopters came and went less often. The ever-changing stream of some of the most wealthy, influential people in the Western world continued, but they no longer flew off to ski each day. Instead, they fished for the Dolly Varden and rainbow trout in the shallow, fast-flowing rivers, or else they walked and rode the trails that the spring thaw had uncovered.

The thirty or so horses that had wintered in the shelter of the open-sided barns on either side of the ranch house began to earn their keep, and Mace also came into his own. The wiry old Indian wrangler had a sixth sense about the whereabouts of game and, day after day, hard-nosed, tough tycoons came back like schoolboys with stories of bighorn sheep and mountain goats seen in the distance and of grizzly bears rearing up from the cover of scrub willow and then turning and shambling rapidly away for the sole benefit, it seemed, of the Leicas and the Nikons focussed on them.

'Y'all mean to say you've never been out on the trail, Mizz Haultain?' One of the millionaire schoolboys asked the question when Kyle returned the full-size

colour prints that had been developed in the ranch's
darkroom in the time between him getting back late
that afternoon and coming down for the usual ritual of
pre-dinner cocktails.

Getting their pictures back so quickly, she had
noticed, seemed to intensify the wilderness experience,
making it one that men who had probably not seen
anything more savage than their wife's pet poodle in
the last ten years were never likely to forget.

The man in question now looked at her, surprised,
over his photographs and bourbon glass. 'You've never
been out on the trail?'

'No, I'm afraid I haven't,' Kyle smiled neutrally.
One of her main duties was to smile, no matter how
much the personality of the recipient grated. And some
of them did. Loud and noisy, setting her nerves on
edge and—she was certain—also grating on Fier. 'I
don't have time.' It was partly true. A million and one
duties almost consumed her day, but Fier went out
with the visitors on the trail. It was that part of her life
at Faucon d'Or that was bearable.

'Nonsense!' The confidence of a successful self-made
man was in the one short word. This was no Stan
Reynolds or Merle Hubbard with the power to make
his presence felt halfway round the world, but he
owned a chain of fried chicken franchises spread all
across North America and was widely known for his
philanthropy. Now he suddenly looked past Kyle's
shoulder. 'I've been telling your Mizz Haultain she
should come out on the trail with us.'

'Why not?' The voice came from behind her and
Kyle spun round, totally surprised.

'*Your* Mizz Haultain!' Even the connotations of the
casual phrase failed to register as cobalt eyes flicked

over her above a smiling mouth.

For once, she had had no idea Fier was so close, and a whole mixture of reaction sprang into life beneath the patterned crêpe of the dinner dress she had bought on her first trip to Edmonton. She had gone mad, she sometimes thought. That dress and two others; skirts and a choice of blouses. She had even bought jeans with the freedom that her credit card had given her and high-heeled cowboy boots, decorated with rows of tripled stitching. The bill had been enormous, but, even with the allowance she sent off to Grace, Fier's cheque at the end of her first month's work had more than covered it.

The labourer was worthy of her hire, Fier had said caustically when she had protested. He paid his staff; they didn't work for free. She had taken the cheque under the sharp reminder of his reality, and the two that had followed it. Of course she was just a member of his staff.

And it was as a member of his staff that he once more silenced her as she tried to talk her way out of the trail ride. The ranch ran smoothly. No one person was indispensable and, ran the implicit warning in those cobalt eyes, no one either argued or let their feelings show in front of guests. 'Charlene can take over for a day or two,' he ordered flatly. 'I'll tell Mace to saddle you a horse.'

Her fingers were cramped from writing reams of notes for her substitute when Kyle finally ran out of excuses to keep her in her office any longer and went reluctantly out into the crisp air the following morning. June in the Rockies was still cold until the sun rose above the mountain tops, and wisps of her breath floated in the air ahead of her. The wranglers, busy cinching the high Western saddles into place or balancing the loads for the packhorses, wore quilted vests over their shirts and jeans, and Kyle wished her earlier extravagance had extended to something warmer than the denim jacket she wore over the plainest of her shirts.

Otherwise, in her jeans and boots and broad brimmed hat, she supposed she looked much like the other guests, a 'dude' ready with her camera for her first excursion into the wilderness.

She had seen it before, of course, the grouping of pack and riding horses on the natural plateau underneath the house with the cowboys moving quietly among them. But now the difference was that she was to be a part of it. It was no longer a question of standing at a window or a door as the horses and their riders set off in single file down the track leading even further into the wilderness of Faucon d'Or. She was not only going with them, she was going to be with Fier.

She could see him now; tall and eye-catching in the universal uniform of jeans and denim jacket and thick quilted vest. Just like the other wranglers, but somehow one apart, with the fallen tail feathers of an eagle slanting down towards his shoulders from the hatband of his hat emphasising not just his leadership but his kinship with the lonely, wild high country.

And hers were not the only eyes to be drawn in his direction. The Chicken King—Harley Davis; out of well-established habit, Kyle mentally recalled the name—had brought a wife with him. Seeing Fier, she had headed straight towards him, all squeals and high-pitched chatter, and she was clinging to him now, drawing out the moment, as he lifted her into her high Western saddle. With her white satin blouse stretched over her ample chest, and her constantly moving, brightly red-lipsticked mouth, she could easily be mistaken for one of the huge plastic chickens her husband had revolving over his franchised diners, Kyle thought sourly. Another sensation that had come into her life since she had come to Faucon d'Or once more swept insidiously through her. It was jealousy—and she had never known how awful it could be.

'Mizz Haultain!' Mace distracted her attention and Fier and the empty-headed woman laughing coyly down at him became just two more people in the moving crowd. 'Mizz Haultain, your horse is over there!'

Riding the trail down from the plateau beneath the ranch was like riding to the edge of nowhere and tipping off. By the time Kyle had regained her balance and looked back, the huge log cabin of the ranch house had already disappeared and there was nothing behind them except a sheer wall of rock, touched with white where snow still lingered in the crevices, and nothing ahead except a broad, smiling valley beckoning them on towards still more massive peaks.

A group of fifteen people and thirty horses had been dwarfed into insignificance and high above them, outstretched pinions glinting in the sun, a bird soared and spiralled in the warming currents of clear air. A golden eagle; the bird of Faucon d'Or.

'It's something else, isn't it?' They had no sooner reached the floor of the first high mountain valley than the Chicken King took advantage of the widening of the track and pushed his horse up beside her.

'Yes, it is,' Kyle answered, but she felt resentful. She didn't want to talk. It was enough to ride; adjusting to an almost forgotten sensation of early childhood, and absorb the immensity of her surroundings. Her eyes needed time. They had never seen such scenery that, on one hand, held the vastness of the mountains and on the other, a miniaturist's patchwork of tiny alpine flowers studding the tenacious wiry grass.

There was wild strawberry—and bluebells! Fleshier than those in England but bluebells, just the same. Those she could identify. The others were just flowers; yellow, white, pink and flaming scarlet, but all incredibly small and delicate to have survived the crushing winter cold.

'I told Cailloux he'd never get me here, but he not only did, he got me back again!'

'Really?' The Chicken King was not to be discouraged and Kyle gave up her attempt. For a short while, she had even forgotten about Fier, but now he sprang into sudden prominence, riding three or four ahead of her on a young brown quarter horse with the Chicken King's wife beside him. A little ache formed in her chest.

'Yup!' It obviously wasn't enough to look the part in an oversize white Stetson and flashy inlaid leather boots from which Mace had firmly removed swan-necked, rowelled spurs before they started; her *compadre* from the gulches of the world of popular mass catering clearly had to sound the part as well. 'Yup!' he went on in his Gary Cooper imitation. 'I came last year and this year I brought Myrna. She was just as leery as I was to begin with, but will y'all just look at her now. She sure is lapping it all up!'

Kyle didn't have to look—she could hear. The nasal, mid-Western voice going on ahead of her with Fier just listening and occasionally interjecting a short remark with his own quiet private smile. How could he bear the almost glutinous attention of a woman like Myrna Davis, with her never-ending stream of silly chatter and her look of schoolgirl worship on her inappropriately over-painted face? And that wasn't jealousy, Kyle told herself. It was part of something that had puzzled her since her very first evening at Faucon d'Or.

She was no nearer understanding now than she had been then just why Fier had decided to open up his own private wilderness to these people. It was true that all of them were rich or, in some way, influential, but they were spoiled and silly, some of them, making even his face harden sometimes with the outrageousness of their demands. And he had no need. His own feeling of self was so complete that he hardly needed the reflected glory of mixing with the rich and powerful to bolster his esteem. He was also rich—a fact Grace had started to point out from the night the hired Mercedes had been so casually discarded and the chauffeur-driven limousine had been summoned to take the three of them to see Thea in her play in London—and the prices charged at Faucon d'Or barely came close to covering expenses. After three months with the books, Kyle was well aware of that.

She sighed, regretting what would have otherwise been the perfect peace of this remote high country, and returned half her attention to the still talking Chicken King riding at her side. Fier must have his reasons for inviting people like Harley Davis to come to Faucon d'Or, but she doubted he would ever uncover them to her. Just as she doubted she would ever know why, when he could have found someone quite easily in Canada, he had gone to the trouble of bringing her from England to replace the ubiquitous Marsha Vincey.

But perhaps her attraction had been her lack of it! Her predecessor's good looks and the use she made of them were by now an open secret among the staff. So, also, was the scene with Fier that had preceded her abrupt dismissal. Presumably by bringing the commonplace woman he remembered over from England, Fier had thought he had solved that problem. How was he to know that his departure from Dovercourt had left her reluctant to fade back into the wallpaper? One day she must tell him—Kyle smiled. Doing it was so unlikely!

But what she would tell him, if she ever found the nerve, was that you couldn't shake up someone's perception of themself—change them into Cinderella for a night—and then expect them to go on as if nothing had ever taken place.

She had been forced back into the position of running Dovercourt—until Fier had appointed young Ted Sully, who else had there been?—but the old self-effacing Kyle had never quite reappeared. Instead of owning just one lipstick, she had found herself using her small amount of available spending money to buy and experiment with cosmetics. Her hair had been taken to the stylist and cut to shoulder length so that it could either be worn up in the soft Victorian fashion that complemented the quiet intelligence of her unusual sherry eyes or, as now, tied back with a broad ribbon so that the fine bones of her face stood out, clear and unencumbered, under the broad brim of her cowboy hat.

What a shock it must have been when Fier walked into his eyrie of a den on that first day and found, not the old Kyle he must have been expecting, but someone subtly different. A woman who had found if not herself, at least an inkling of what that self could be. No more wallpaper—certainly not in that black dress! After three whole months she could still cringe when she remembered the episode that dress had led to with Merle Hubbard. The billionaire had made no secret of his interest—and nor had Fier. But his concern had been with the reputation of Faucon d'Or, not with her changed image. He still rarely spoke to her except when it was unavoidable. Still, mercifully, had no idea what those few moments in his arms had done to her.

'Myrna's been telling me I should run some kinda promotional deal,' the Chicken King beside her was going on. 'Chicken in the Wilderness—that sorta thing! What do y'all think?'

Having found an audience he stayed relentlessly at her side, elaborating on a scheme which somehow had purchasers of the super-jumbo size barrel of fried chicken competing to eat it in the wilderness.

'And picking up their trash afterwards,' he added. 'Can't have any of that left around!'

'Maybe you could give a Wilderness Holiday as a prize to any group collecting the most rubbish in their community,' Kyle suggested half seriously.

'Say! Whaddya think of that!' His eyes opened in genuine admiration. 'They'd have to buy the barrel first, of course, to be eligible to compete, but you've sure got something there! There's a brain behind that face of yours, pretty lady!'

He talked through lunch and through the afternoon and it was almost a relief to reach the camp that had been the main cause of Kyle's reluctance to join this particular excursion.

This was one of the overnight trail rides, designed

to give the pampered guests of Faucon d'Or a longer experience of the wilderness. Sleeping in tents located at discreet intervals among the trees and eating fresh trout, caught by the wranglers and cooked over a wood fire. The wine was there; the high standard of service was the same, but it was organised by Mace and, with nothing to do and no responsibilities, Kyle found herself in the position of another guest. No—not a guest! A woman with no hope that he would even notice her forced into the company of the man she lóved for forty-eight long hours.

It stayed light in the high country. At ten o'clock, the sun was only just dipping towards the mountain tops and at ten o'clock, Kyle stood beside the rushing shallow water of the Berlin river and watched it finally begin to set.

Unable to bear the noise and chatter of the campfire, she had slipped unobtrusively away—looking for quiet; looking to escape. It was more than she could bear to stay there watching him; physically so close but otherwise so far apart.

Tired of its long, eighteen-hour midsummer day, the sun dropped quickly. In a few minutes it was dark—or as dark as it would ever get at that time of the year—and there was only the whiteness of the water left.

'The young years!' The voice came from the shadow of the trees behind her. She thought she had escaped, but she had not! Every fibre of her body registered. He could see her, she supposed, outlined against the river, but she was safe. She started to relax her guard. He couldn't possibly have seen her swift reaction or heard the way her breath caught swiftly in her throat. Convinced, she slowly swung around to face him. 'Don't you see them?' he enquired on a quiet breath.

No, she couldn't see anything. All there was was the fluid strength of the figure approaching her with silent footsteps across the deep green moss—part-Cree, part-Iroquois, her mind subconsciously recalled—and, in a quirk of light reflected from the river, a hint of cobalt deep in luminous eyes.

It had been those eyes resting dispassionately upon her that had driven her away from camp. They saw and guessed too much; might even guess the foolish jealousy that consumed her as the Chicken King's chicken-headed wife had gazed adoringly up at him under her husband's benignant gaze. And now, in seeking to escape, she was alone with him.

'Look—over there!' He reached her and his arm went round her waist, not to draw her to him but to turn her in the direction of a mountain fir that had fallen across the river to make a natural bridge. There, half hidden by the branches stirred by the late evening breeze, she could see two figures. Fier had immediately picked them out. She had not. Two almost adult teenage children brought by their families, and now, like her, escaping from the campfire to be alone. 'Do you see them now?' Fier asked her softly.

'Yes.' His touch had brought her every sense alive. Sight, smell, hearing; a landscape that had been featureless since the sun had disappeared was now full of detail. 'But not until you showed me,' she added honestly.

She felt him smile. 'Let's walk,' he said. 'There's no need to disturb them.'

She must be dreaming and would have known she was except for the total reality of the small night sounds of the mountains—a sleepy bird, a rustle disappearing in the undergrowth—as he led her along the bank until a slight bend in the river hid the tree from sight. She would also know she was living in a fantasy if it hadn't been for the continuing gentle pressure of Fier's hand against her waist. But although she wasn't dreaming, in a moment, she would wake. Fier was never gentle. He was scathing, aloof, amused. He was many things— she shivered at the memory of his anger—but he was never gentle; not with her. The only time she ever saw the other side of the multi-faceted coin that was his personality was when he was with Mace. The old Indian wrangler was the only one who seemed to have a special place in that otherwise impassive heart.

'Are you cold?' Her shudder at the uncalled memory of the angry scene over Merle Hubbard had transmitted itself through the strong brown fingers resting on her waist and he was already stripping off the quilted down-filled vest he wore over his plaid shirt to drape around her shoulders.

'No ... I....' The gleam in the eyes above her warned her. Don't prevaricate! 'Thank you!' She *was* cold, she had been standing beside the river for longer than she had thought. 'What did you mean?' she asked eventually. 'The young years?'

'What?' He looked confused. Another first; Fier Cailloux never looked confused. But she had to do something—say something to dispel the almost overwhelming impression of being in his arms as she took the vest that held his warmth and drew it tight around her. 'Ah, yes!' In the light of a high northern summer night which was never entirely dark, the carved face above her cleared. 'The young years! Seeing those two,' he nodded in the direction of the fallen tree with its burden of young lovers, 'reminded me of what I can never have.'

He had everything and yet he had regret. She didn't understand. It was also light enough for him to see her expression of surprise.

'I'm thirty-eight. I'll never have the time again that those two have ahead of them.' He once more nodded back towards the tree.

And she was twenty-nine. Another birthday had come and gone, unnoticed by everyone else, maybe, but not by her, since she had arrived at Faucon d'Or. The tender years—what had Fier called them?

Standing there, looking up at him, touched by the unexpected vulnerability of the lock of dark hair falling across his forehead, her exact memory had gone, but she knew what he meant. The future might hold many things for both of them, but one thing they could neither of them have was the joy of love that started young and proceeded without hindrance to fulfilment.

'Are you envious?' she asked him quietly.

'A little! Who wouldn't be?' She saw his rueful smile. 'But time passing is something no one can control.'

'But surely you can control what you do with it!' And she had not done that, she realised. She had drifted, letting Grace and Thea do the living for her until it was too late. Fier himself had been the one to point that out and now, at twenty-nine, she was having her first experience of love with a man who, except on this precious rare occasion, had barely said two personal words to her since the night he had forcibly dragged her away from Merle Hubbard's door.

'Sure, you can control some things in your life.' He was looking into the distance above her head. 'You can go away, leave where you were born, set up a new life. You can have affairs; you can even fall in love and then realise when it comes to making that love permanent that it would never work. That Paris and the wilderness will never mix.'

'She lived in Paris?' She had always known that there had to be someone. A man like Fier, with passions running so close beneath the surface of his skin, could never have gone through so much of his adult life untouched.

'She still does.' His downward glance made her heart clench. 'She's married to a judge and, at the last count, there were two children. But that's water under the bridge,' he nodded in the direction of the fallen tree with a little smile. 'It took a lot of anguish, but I'm pleased now it's like that.' No regrets—that wouldn't be his way. A decision had been made and put behind him. 'I can see now that I was already being pulled back here when we met. I'd tried to break the ties, leave Faucon d'Or, go into business—be anything but what I am, but the direction I had to take had already been laid down for me.'

For her, maybe, but surely not for him? He had the means, the strength of will, to shape his life in any way he chose. She was the one who had been trapped by heritage until Dovercourt had passed into the hands of the man now facing her.

'When I inherited all this,' his look took in the trees, the sky, the almost invisible mountains in the darkness, 'I knew that what I had was only a small part of something that was already on its way to being totally destroyed!' The voice that had earlier been burred and gentle now started to turn harsh and the man she knew—grandson of that Indian boy who had run for seven days and seven nights to reclaim his heritage— was once more standing over her.

'Progress,' he made it sound like rape, 'was slashing

and burning its way into the wilderness. In ten years, maybe twenty, it would all be destroyed—or tamed! Picnic tables, camping sites—wild life permitted to exist for the sake of weekend photographers!' He was talking about what was offered at Faucon d'Or, but there was an edge. 'So I decided to join the "progressives" at their own game. To give the right people an experience of the wilderness that they would take away and use their power to preserve. That's where my young years went,' he slackened as if suddenly remembering she was there. 'Turning a small hunting lodge into a luxury resort; bringing everything piece by piece up to the mountain and then seducing the right people to use their influence to preserve not only my wilderness,' his lips twisted in a smile against himself, 'but all the untamed, unexploited space that still exists.'

It all fell into place. Questions that she had been asking herself almost since the moment she had arrived had been answered with a passionate force. She and the man standing in front of her with that rueful smile still curving his thin dark lips were so much the same— and yet they were so different. Fier had given his young years to an ideal. She had let hers drift away. Was that less destructive? Or was it more? She didn't know. All she knew was that his passion had struck an answering chord which made it quite impossible for her to go on standing there—and quite impossible for her to turn away.

'Kyle!' In the semi-darkness, his voice lapped round her, touching her heated forehead with his breath.

'I have to go.' Her own voice sounded jerky; choked. Something she had dreamed of was going to happen— and she was terrified.

It was the aftermath of strong emotion; it was the solitude. It was part of his nostalgia of regret for those young years. It was anything and everything except a need for her that was making him draw her gently into his arms.

She tried to tell herself, tried to use the humiliation of those never-to-be-forgotten moments on that first night when he had aroused a hunger in her body just to punish her, but it was no use. This time the hands that held her were sliding gently down her spine and the featherlight touch of the mouth that had once so angrily attacked her was robbing her of all will.

'Fee-air! Oh, Fee-air! Is that you down there?' The voice and the footsteps of the Chicken King's feather-headed wife came crashing through the undergrowth towards them just as his mouth was starting to move more sensuously against her, drawing gasps of painlike pleasure as it forced her lips to part. 'Oh, Fee-air! Monsieur Kye-oo!'

It was cold as his arms released her and the night air struck her face; cold and somehow desolate as he held her at arm's length, his body bowstring taut and his dark eyes furious.

'Damn!' he whispered angrily. 'Damn!' he said.

CHAPTER SIX

'WELL, what did you expect me to do?' Grace asked pettishly. 'Trail round Europe after Fred and Buffy and all that crowd like some sort of beggar without a penny to my name?'

No, she wouldn't expect Grace to do that, Kyle thought privately, but the last thing she had expected was ever to see her sitting in Fier's private den at Faucon d'Or with the mountains forming a background to her own particular startling brand of golden loveliness.

'I am *homeless*, you know, in case it had escaped you!' Grace pointed out. 'I didn't have anyone falling over themselves to offer *me* a job when we lost Dovercourt!'

'But. . . .' Kyle got the one word in.

'Oh, I know, I know!' Grace waved an airy hand. 'You sent me what you could—and I'm grateful, I really am.' She gave the dazzling smile that made everyone forgive her. 'But life's so expensive nowadays. I just don't know where money goes!' Try holidays and expensive clothes, Kyle thought. Grace's ultra-fashionable summer suit was obviously new. 'I did try, I really did to economise, but there's a limit to the amount of time one can go on inviting oneself to stay with friends! And then when I'm finally forced to go back to England or become the laughing stock of the better part of Europe, I find that oaf Ted Sully's been put in charge. You really should have told me about that, you know, Kylie,' she finished plaintively.

She had. She had included Fier's decision to appoint Ted Sully to manage Dovercourt in the letter she had written to tell Grace about her own departure for Canada. But then when had Grace ever bothered to read letters unless the contents were of immediate concern to her? And that particular letter must have arrived when she had been in the thick of the fashionable skiing season at Klosters.

'I'm sorry.' How easy it was to go back to the position of being the one automatically in the wrong! Kyle gave a rueful little smile. She thought she had, but she really hadn't changed that much.

'It's all right, I forgive you,' Grace said graciously. She glanced into the gold-fitted alligator bag on the couch beside her. 'Do you think you could find me a cigarette?—Thanks.' She took one from the box Kyle brought across to her, lit it with a slim gold lighter and coughed. 'God, this must be antique! Doesn't anyone smoke around here?' She studied the burning tip, took two more puffs and stubbed it out. 'Anyway—where was I? Oh, yes. When I got back to Dovercourt, that idiot Sully——' one of the few who had never been totally captivated by Grace's charm, as Kyle recalled, '—made it quite clear that I wasn't wanted. And Thea was no better!'

'You saw her, then?' Kyle had only heard once from their glamorous mother and that, strangely enough, had been a letter of wild approval for her changed circumstances.

'Of course I saw her,' Grace snapped. 'Where else was I to go? She's finished the Shaw play and now she's talking about doing a film somewhere. I thought she might have wangled me a part in it, to say the least, she didn't seem too keen. Probably because of

George. Oh, didn't you know?' Grace read the question forming in Kyle's eyes. 'Our respected mother's got this new young man. George Something—quite dishy, actually! Certainly a cut above some of the awful creeps she's had in the past. Older, too. Anyway,' the gleam that had appeared in the beautiful violet eyes snapped out, 'Thea gave me a thousand pounds and told me to get lost!'

'She what?' Kyle was amazed.

'That's right.' Grace looked satisfied. 'She didn't actually say as much, but she made it quite clear that there wasn't room for the two of us in the flat with the lovely George around, and more or less marked the way to the door with neon signs!'

Kyle found it difficult to believe. Grace was the favourite: Thea would never leave her without anywhere to turn. 'She must have suggested something!'

'She did. She said in no uncertain terms that I should go back to Alex.'

'Oh, I see.' There was a silence. 'And are you going to?' There had been nothing further on that subject since Grace's first and only letter.

'Of course I'm not!' Grace snapped. 'I daresay he'd be pleased enough to see me, but why should I go back to Alex when there might be something else? How are you getting on with him, by the way?'

'Getting on with who?' Kyle asked the question but it was a mere formality. The sinking feeling round her heart told her that she perfectly well knew who.

'Fier, of course. Our lovely cousin twice removed— or however many times it is. Don't be so dense, Kylie! Who else could I mean?' She sank back into the luxurious leather padding of the couch and looked around Fier's private den with a sigh of quiet approval. 'I must say I didn't expect it to be so lush here. Quite a surprise!' She reached for another cigarette. 'Well, come on, then,' she prompted. 'Tell me. How are you getting on with him?'

'I work for him,' Kyle said stiffly. 'We don't have to "get on".'

Grace's eyes narrowed through the plume of smoke. 'Has anyone ever told you you're turning quite tricky in your old age?' she remarked quietly. 'I wonder why?'

Why indeed? Why was she being so evasive about her relationship with Fier?—or tricky, as Grace put it. All there had been had been those few moments beside the Berlin river; a feeling of being let into Fier's confidence; a feeling of being someone special, someone cherished, as his arms had swept around her. For a few days the afterglow of those moments had continued, but then, as nothing had been said or done to prove they hadn't been a dream, the old familiar doubts had begun to filter back.

It was true Fier had been more approachable, less remote. For part of the way back from the overnight camp, he had even ridden alongside her, pointing out things her novice eyes had missed. The freshly turned earth where a grizzly bear had dug for roots beside the trail and the flick of a furry rodent body as they once more left the valley and climbed above the tree line towards the ranch and a colony of striped pikas had dived for cover in their burrows in the shale.

Her pleasure had been reflected in his face, drawing them closer, giving them a common bond of delight in the untamed wilderness, but once the ride was over, once the demands of the everyday routine of Faucon d'Or had claimed them, it became more and more difficult to believe that those incidents had ever happened or that the episode beside the Berlin river had ever taken place.

Fier was pleasant, smiling sometimes, even sharing a moment of wry humour the day before when the Chicken King's fluffy wife had been making her extravagant farewells and his eye had caught Kyle's over the elaborately windblown hairstyle. But seeing that quiet glint in darker cobalt, Kyle had frozen. She had known that she was doing it, but she couldn't stop. The defence mechanism she had developed through the years had been too strong.

She could never go back to being exactly what she was but letting her emotions show was too dangerous— too fraught with pain. Memories of the father who, at times, seemed to have had trouble remembering she existed were still too close and if, as she suspected, Fier was regretting her that glimpse of the passionate human being underneath the normally impervious facade, she would be wise to do as he was. Pretend that it had never happened.

So she had smiled neutrally back at him across the windblown hairstyle and turned away across the helipad.

And now Grace had arrived. Totally unexpectedly; claiming a spare seat when the helicopter had flown in from Edmonton with two new guests that afternoon. A lump formed behind Kyle's breastbone. With all she knew—with all that life had taught her—why was she even bothering to be what Grace called 'tricky'?

'So? What's the big secret?' Grace now mocked her. 'Don't tell me I wasn't too far off the mark when I suggested you should marry him!'

'Grace!' Kyle flushed. 'You're being ridiculous!'

'Am I?' The perfect sickle moons of eyebrows rose. 'From the look of you, I can't see you actually kicking and screaming your way up the aisle! Oh, well,' she leaned forward to the ashtray, 'if you won't tell me what's going on, I'll have to find out, I guess. It shouldn't be too difficult.'

Nothing was. Not if you were Grace.

'How long are you going to be staying here?' Kyle abruptly changed the subject.

'That depends.' Grace straightened slowly. 'I don't know yet how long I'll want to—or how long I'll be invited.' The lump behind Kyle's breastbone turned to lead and Grace gave a crow of triumph. 'I told you I'd find out! You should just see your face! You've fallen, haven't you? My God, I never thought I'd live to see the day! My little elder sister's fallen off her pedestal!'

'I don't know what you mean. . . .' Kyle started, but Grace interrupted her.

'Oh, don't worry, I won't tell him——' she paused with a long silence, '—yet.'

'Grace?' Another voice came into that long silence. Doubtful, tinged—remarkably—with displeasure.

Black hair, dark face, bone and sinew stretching the denim of his Levis and open-collared shirt, and the glint of a thick gold chain showing against the tanned skin of his chest. Grace's eyes widened, but Kyle's breath caught quickly in her throat. Fier was standing in the open doorway and she had no idea how long he'd been there.

'She came this afternoon. She was in Edmonton and I thought that as the helicopter was going in anyway. . . .' Kyle launched into a hurried justification.

Anything, but anything, to distract his attention from what he might have heard.

'Are the LaRocques settled in?' he cut across her, his first concern the French Canadian politician and his wife who had been the reason for the helicopter going in to Edmonton.

'Of course. They're upstairs, taking a nap.' He was annoyed, of course, because she had brought Grace to his private quarters. That accounted for the hardening of the bones beneath the impassive sculpture of his face. This was the first time she had been there herself since the day she had arrived. It was private, guarded, his place to be alone, with its view across the mountains to the distant peaks of Gunsite Pass. But her office was too small and she hadn't thought, until this moment, of taking Grace up to her room.

'Now you're not to blame poor Kylie! It's your fault, anyway!' Grace was coming to her rescue, standing, gracefully, from the chesterfield and walking towards Fier. 'How could she possibly refuse to let me come when she knew I was in Edmonton without a penny to my name?'

And how could Grace know the real cause of Fier's annoyance? Kyle thought fleetingly. No one ever grudged her entry anywhere. It was hopeless. Thank God she hadn't been fool enough to let her feelings show. Now that Grace was here, Fier wouldn't be giving her a second look.

'Hallo, Fier.' Grace's speech had taken her across the room and now she stood there, looking up at him. Kyle couldn't see her face; she didn't have to. She could see Fier's. He might have looked annoyed when he first came in but now he was softening, smiling, bending down to brush his lips across Grace's softly tinted cheek.

'Grace!' The voice held no hint of what he must be thinking. If anything, Grace was even more beautiful. 'And what are you doing here?'

'Darling!' Grace was aggrieved. 'I thought this was my home! You took the only one I had, remember?'

'But you can live at Dovercourt any time you choose.'

'Then you'd better tell Ted Sully that!' Grace answered sharply. 'He practically threw me out!'

So much for poor Ted Sully! When Fier had offered him the opportunity to manage the estate, he had probably thought his chance had come. But no one fought and won with Grace. Ted would soon be looking for another opening.

'Really?' Fier's dry voice confirmed Kyle's intuition. 'Now, tell me, what's my fault and not Kyle's?'

'It was your fault that I had to hang around in Edmonton for hours.' Grace took his arm and turned and *now* Kyle could see her face—beautiful, beguiling, innocent. 'If you'd been here when I got a message through, you could have flown down and collected me yourself. As it was, I had to wait for ever! And then, when that pilot of yours finally found me, he said he hadn't got room for all my luggage!'

'I'll send him back tomorrow!'

Was she imagining the irony? Of course not, Kyle decided.

'Will you, darling?' Grace clung to him. 'I know it's silly,' she drew a shaky breath, 'but what's in those cases is all I've got left in the whole world! I can't explain, but Kyle knows what I mean.' She threw her sister an appealing glance.

She was being used, Kyle realised, and there was nothing she could do to stop it.

Another pair of eyes switched to her, dark and expressionless. 'In that case, Kyle will probably be happy to arrange for Mike to fly in and pick them up.'

'Of course,' Kyle answered through stiff lips, hating herself. Why was she being so resentful? Grace was her *sister*!

'Have you had anything to eat or drink?' With Grace once more on the chesterfield, Fier stood over her.

'Yes, Kyle got me some tea.'

The admirable Kyle. Efficient, self-effacing. Good to fetch and carry; the perfect foil for Grace. She didn't know why she was even bothering to be what Grace called 'tricky'. Grace had already guessed she was in love with Fier—what else had she got to hide?

'Good.' Fier stood smiling down at Grace a moment longer and then he turned towards an inlaid cabinet. 'And now I think we all deserve a drink before we change for dinner. Scotch? Bourbon?'

'Scotch, please,' said Grace with a look at Kyle.

Dimly aware of the chink of decanter against cut glasses and of the conversation continuing in the background, Kyle stood there numbly.

Even if Fier had once permitted her a glimpse of the man behind the normally impassive façade, what difference did that make? With Grace now on the scene, he was hardly likely to give her a second glance.

She remembered the camellias—the first time she had thought of them in months. When Fier had given her that black dress, she had thought—Heaven knew what she had thought!—and then Grace had come down the stairs at Dovercourt with his blush camellias nestled in her hair and everything had fallen into place.

For her there had been a gift to change the image of

a dull and dowdy woman with whom, for politeness' sake, he was being obliged to spend the evening. For Grace, it had been a tribute to the beauty that had already made its mark.

'Kyle!' Fier spoke to her and the amber liquid in the glass that had materialised in her hand tilted dangerously as she came to with a start. 'The suite at the top of the stairs—it's empty, isn't it?'

It took her a second or two to realise, then, 'Yes . . . Yes, it is.'

'Then put Grace in there.' He gave the golden-haired woman on the couch in front of him an enigmatic glance. 'Having stolen her home away from her, we must do what we can to make her comfortable.'

'I don't want to put you to any trouble!' This time, Grace had also heard the faintly mocking edge.

'On the contrary——' Fier looked at her and then at Kyle, 'Kyle will see you settled in. Incidentally,' he paused on his way to the cabinet to replace his empty glass, 'how long do you plan to stay?'

'I don't know yet.' Grace looked uncomfortable. 'Does it matter?'

'No, of course not.' The fine American crystal rang as it went down on the silver tray. 'I was just wondering how you were going to keep yourself amused. I hardly think you'll want to come out on the trail!'

'No.' Grace frowned, then brightened. 'I know, I could help Kyle. Not at housekeeping—I'm not much good at that—but I could be your hostess.' In other words, she could stay in the background while Grace took her accustomed place centre stage, Kyle realised. 'I *am* good at making sure people enjoy themselves!' Grace finished brightly.

'Yes.' In the act of turning towards the door, Fier

paused and the sunlight streaming in through the picture window etched a wry twist to his face. 'Yes, I'm sure you are. And now, if you'll forgive me, I have to go and change.' He nodded towards Kyle. 'Don't stay too long talking!'

'*What* were you saying about me going back to Alex?' The door had barely closed before Grace lay back on the sofa with the half smile of a contented cat on her beautifully heart-shaped face.

'I didn't say anything,' Kyle pointed out. 'You were the one who mentioned it.'

'Good!' Grace stretched and purred. 'Then don't.'

Kyle felt the first faint stirrings of real premonition. 'You don't mean to say you really are going to stay on here indefinitely?'

'Why not? Do you know,' Grace nodded in the direction of the closed door, 'I'd actually forgotten what he was like! And to think I wasted all those months trailing around Europe when I could have been here all the time! Kylie,' she noticed the expression on Kyle's face, 'please don't look so miserable. All's fair in love and war! You've had a clear field with him all these months and you haven't got very far now, have you, darling?'

No, she hadn't. And even if she had, that wouldn't have stopped Grace. Taking Fier away from her would just have added spice. Now all she had to worry about was if Grace would tell Fier what she had found out. She didn't think she could bear it if he knew she was in love with him.

'Oh, I know I've got some work to do,' Grace said reflectively. 'Even I could tell he wasn't exactly overjoyed to see me! But he'll come round.' She shot Kyle a diamond glance. 'They always do!'

'Okay, now tell me the real story.' In her office the following morning, Fier was filling it both physically and mentally.

He was leaning against the edge of her metal desk—her office was so small, where else was he to go?—but it put his thigh only inches away from her.

'The real story about what?' His eyes, unseen but felt, were drilling through her skull.

'About your sister.' He should have said Grace; not talked about her as someone he scarcely knew.

'She told you.' Kyle did her best to sound controlled. 'She came here because she had nowhere else to go.'

'Yes——' a hand came out and picked one of the invoices from the pile in front of her, '—I heard the orphan of the storm routine.' The invoice came back with a finger pointing to a totalled figure. 'This amount is wrong.'

She couldn't take her eyes away. 'I'll query it,' she said jerkily.

'Good!' The finger disappeared. 'Did you invite her here?'

'Who? Grace?' Surprise made her look up. His face was dark and hard under its mane of jet black hair. She looked away, frightened by her response. 'No.' He could hardly know how little she would want to ask Grace to come to Faucon d'Or. 'The first thing I knew was when I got a message that she was waiting at the airport in Edmonton. She said I was her last hope.'

'I see.' The voice was flat. 'I'm surprised she didn't stay on with Thea. I can see why Dovercourt on her own wouldn't have too much appeal——' So Ted Sully was to get a reprieve after all. It has also crossed Kyle's mind that the reason for Grace's refusal to stay on at

Dovercourt might have had less to do with Ted Sully's lack of enthusiasm than the prospect of staying there alone. Grace needed an audience if she was to come into her own, and she had certainly had one at Faucon d'Or the previous night.

At dinner, candlelight catching her blonde hair and making her violet eyes huge and mysterious and afterwards, taking Kyle's place behind the coffee tray as if by right and generally holding court.

The room had been divided in two camps: women on one side and men around the chesterfield and when Kyle, her place usurped and nothing left to do, had slipped unobtrusively away, Grace had been sitting on the chesterfield holding court to an admiring circle.

If she had been setting out to prove just how useful she could be as his hostess, she must have succeeded beyond her wildest dreams. On her way upstairs, Kyle had also seen the speculative, thoughtful look on Fier's face.

'So why wouldn't Grace stay with Thea?' In her office the following morning Fier, for some reason of his own, seemed determined to pursue the point.

Kyle shifted uncomfortably. 'They don't always see eye to eye.' Not when Thea hadn't consolidated her position and sensed competition for one of her 'young men'. And that must have been exactly what had happened in the flat in Curzon Street, if the normally penny-pinching Thea had been prepared to disburse a thousand pounds to persuade Grace to leave. But she had no need to dot the i's and cross the t's. Kyle picked up another one of the invoices on her desk.

There was also no need to tell him what Grace's opinion was likely to be about living permanently in the wilderness. He had told her how he had turned his back on love once for the sake of Faucon d'Or. But he was older now—and Grace was Grace.

'I see.' Fier sounded satisfied. 'Which seems to leave us with Orsinski. What about him?'

'I don't know.'

'Will you please look at me when I talk to you!' The hand that had pointed out the error on the invoice now went underneath her chin, forcing her to face him. 'Where's Orsinski now?' he asked.

'He's in the South of France.' Kyle wrenched her face away. It was enough to know that she had lost what she had never had; she didn't have to see how important her answer was to him. And of course Fier was interested in Alex. He was Grace's husband—or would be until the divorce went through. With Alex still legally on the scene, Grace wasn't free. 'I believe he wants her to go back to him, but she's refused.' There—it was out! Like pulling a plaster from an aching wound, it was better to do it with one swift painful tug.

'Have you any idea why she's refused?'

'No. I think she's bored, that's all.' She couldn't be jealous of her sister, but she could be honest.

'With Orsinski or with marriage?'

'With Alex,' Kyle admitted. Why wouldn't he stop questioning her? What else did he want to know? Apparently one more thing.

'Do you have an address for him?' he enquired unexpectedly.

'An address?' The question took her totally by surprise.

'Yes—an address!' His temper, which had been audibly fraying, suddenly snapped. 'Oh, for Pete's sake, Kyle, stop being so obtuse! And while we're at it,

I don't want a repeat of your performance yesterday night. You're here to take care of the welfare of the guests. I will not have you slipping away half way through the evening leaving everything to Grace! Where is she, by the way?'

'I think she's still in bed. I had a breakfast tray sent up to her.' Kyle was suddenly equally furious and her sherry brown eyes snapped as she sat erect and swung to face him. Nothing could hurt her now. What more did she have to lose? 'I'm pleased that at least part of my work here leaves you satisfied!' she said acidly.

It was his turn to look surprised; one eyebrow raising beneath the lock of hair across his forehead.

'It's nice to know that I'm better than Grace at pouring coffee!' she clarified.

'Not better—just different,' he said insufferably. 'You don't turn it into a major production exercise.'

In other words, she was suitably unobtrusive! Or did he mean that Grace's charm and glitter shouldn't be obscured by something as mundane as a coffee tray— even if the tray in question was beautiful antique silver? Either way, the answer rankled.

'Now——' he stood there waiting. If it hadn't been so incredible, she might have thought he smiled. '—I believe you have an address for me!'

'What? Oh, yes.' Feeling considerably deflated, Kyle reached for her pad and scribbled the name of Alexei Orsinski's villa in Cannes. What was he going to do? she wondered. Check her story or tell Alex to stop pestering Grace? After seeing the way he had watched Grace last night, could she really be in any doubt? It was satisfying to rip the page from the pad with a loud tearing noise.

'Thank you.' Fier took the ill-used sheet of paper

from her without a downward glance. 'Have you any idea when Grace will be down? I'd like to see her, and I'm due out fishing with the LaRocques in half an hour.' He moved away from the desk, but even so, the office was so small, his presence touched her.

'I'll send a maid up to her room.' Although whether, even then, Grace would put in an appearance was something that Kyle doubted.

It had been well after two o'clock when she had heard footsteps—two pairs of footsteps—and then laughter and then Grace's voice bidding someone goodnight. She had felt guilty, laying there in bed, ears straining, as if she was checking up on Grace; she had felt even worse when she had realised that the second voice belonged to Fier. The clipped French-sounding accent was easy to recognise even at the distance of a corridor and through her bedroom door.

So Fier and Grace had lingered alone in the lounge downstairs for a last conversation—a last embrace: or what would undoubtedly have been a last embrace if it hadn't been Ben's job to stay on duty until the last person had left.

But, by going to bed at two, Grace was unlikely to put in an appearance before lunchtime no matter who summoned her. And, to be fair—Kyle cursed the mentality that always had her being fair—Grace also had to contend with jet-lag. Kyle remembered what it had done to her. Disorientating her; leaving her totally at a loss until, that was, a hand had snatched hers away from the wrong door handle and propelled her to her room.

'I'll ask Charlene to tell Grace you want to see her,' she repeated woodenly. 'But I don't know if she'll be down.' She again regretted the propensity for fairness that drove her on, but how did you overcome the habit of a lifetime? 'Look after Grace—take care of your baby sister!' Those had been her instructions from the time that Grace was born. Just as it was impossible for her to be jealous of the child and then the woman who had outshone her with other people all her life, it was impossible to stop protecting her. 'She had a long journey yesterday—a late night,' she said to the impassive face of the man still watching her.

'In that case, I'll see her this evening.' She couldn't read his thoughts but she had the uncanny feeling he could read hers. 'Tell her I'll expect her in my office about six.'

Alone in his eyrie of a den, Kyle's imagination involuntarily supplied the intimacy of the rendezvous. 'Yes, of course,' she said.

'Then if there's nothing else?' He stood there watching her.

'No, nothing.' Why wouldn't he just leave? Surely he knew her well enough not to have his eyes range over the figure-fitting outline of her blouse or probe the barely hidden tensions of a face struggling to meet his inspection squarely without protection from the thick mane of sherry-coloured hair clubbed softly back into the nape of her neck with its broad, black velvet ribbon.

He moved towards the door at last and tension ebbed until he opened it and paused on his way through. 'Incidentally,' the light of mockery, it could be nothing else, glinted in his eyes and smile, 'have I told you recently that you've improved?'

The door closed quietly, leaving her alone and in utter silence except for the sound of her breath as she let it go. At least he thought she had improved—whatever that might mean! What was it? Some sort of consolation prize? She was never going to be anything other than unremarkable in looks, but at least she had improved. She no longer avoided any and every confrontation; at least she could sit up straight and look at him. After days of trying to avoid him, trying to forget the might-have-been of those few moments beside a mountain stream before the Chicken King's wife had come blundering in, she could now do that, at least.

And she had to go on doing it for three more months. Half the time her visa allowed her to stay in Canada had expired and in the middle of September, it would be back to Dovercourt—No! She wouldn't be going back to the lush familiarity of the Sussex countryside with its autumn tints. She had forgotten: Dovercourt no longer belonged to them. The last Haultain had gone. For her it would be back to London. To a private hotel first, perhaps, until she found a flat and then a job. And maybe she wouldn't need a flat. With the practical experience she now had, perhaps she could get a job as a housekeeper in some hotel and live in. That would certainly solve the problem of accommodation—and she could deal with her other problems later on.

Knowing Fier, loving Fier, knowing that she could never be the same again. Never be quite as deliberately detached from her emotions or content to live life at second hand. But surely even that would fade. Surely, with time passing, she would slowly go back to being what she had once been. Unobtrusive, unremarkable Kyle Haultain; content to stay on the sidelines of other people's lives.

Maybe, one day, there would even be someone else. Another man to come sweeping into her ordered life, making colours brighter and sensations more acute. She smiled at the improbability and her heart hurt.

Meanwhile—she stretched a hand towards the buzzer on her desk, then let it drop—Grace had to be told that Fier wanted to see her and as she had to go on pretending for the next three months, rather than send Charlene or one of the other maids, she would test her new 'improvement' and go and tell Grace herself.

'Grace! Are you awake?' Kyle knocked and called before she opened the bedroom door, but all she got was silence when she went in.

Grace was fast asleep, on her back, like a child with her blonde hair spread across the pillow on either side of her tranquil face. The only sign that she had ever been awake was the light switched on beside the bed and the half empty glass of fresh squeezed orange juice on the breakfast tray. Otherwise, the tray had not been touched.

Kyle once more felt the old protective surge. Grace looked so vulnerable sleeping there. No wonder Fier was already half in love with her. No wonder he wanted to find out how the situation stood with Alex and just why Grace had come to Faucon d'Or. He had been interested in Grace's plans since the arrival of Grace's one and only letter shortly after Kyle herself had got there.

Grace had really had nowhere else to go. That much, at least, was genuine, and the whys and wherefores were none of Fier's concern. There was no need to explain that she had deliberately provoked Thea into throwing her out of the London flat or that her refusal to go back to Alex was based on sheer caprice. There was also no need to tell Fier that Grace had now deliberately set her sights on him. She looked so innocent. How could he possibly believe it. And even if he did, wouldn't he be overjoyed?

Kyle picked up the breakfast tray, switched off the bedside lamp and walked quietly across the thick pile carpet to the door. Grace could sleep. There was time enough to tell her that Fier wanted to see her later on.

CHAPTER SEVEN

'HE said if I ever did anything remotely like it again, he'd send me away!'

'He said what?' In Grace's room that evening, with a recently tearful Grace, Kyle was sure she had misunderstood.

'He said it was about time I grew up and stopped behaving as if the entire world revolved round me! He said——' her voice began to waver and turn into an injured wail, 'Oh, Kylie, it was awful! He practically accused me of seducing Guy LaRocque. I'd no idea he could be like that!'

She had, Kyle thought. She had also been on the receiving end of one of those crushing bouts of Fier's thin lipped, hard faced displeasure. But probably no one had ever treated Grace like that in her life.

'As if it's my fault the man's married to a frump,' Grace said resentfully, 'or that he wanted to stay on and talk after she'd gone to bed. And it wasn't as if we were ever left alone! Fier was there almost all the time, and then when he got called away, that creep Ben, or whatever he calls himself, was hovering around the place in his white coat, listening to every word. If it hadn't been for him, Fier would probably never have found out. Rotten spy!'

Grace finished on a sullen note, but Kyle was no longer listening. She was reliving two o'clock that morning, hearing two voices coming dimly through the closed door of her room. One Grace's—that was unmistakable—but the other one not Fier's. The light seemed brighter; the upcoming evening less of an ordeal to face. The voice she had heard talking to Grace had belonged to the urbane, grey-haired politician, Guy LaRocque, who had arrived earlier that day on the chopper from Edmonton with his wife—and Grace.

Her mistake was understandable. She had barely exchanged ten words with the Quebec politician since he had arrived and his voice and Fier's were so alike. Both touched with French; both clipped with authority. It was only when the two men were together in the same room that the difference was apparent. One voice holding a politician's practised smoothness, the other sharper edged with an authority that owed no one anything.

'Kylie!' Something in Grace's tone punctured Kyle's irrational bubble of small happiness. 'I've just thought of something! You don't think he was jealous, do you?—Fier, I mean,' she clarified. Like a child's her face had cleared, leaving no sign of recent tears or temper. 'Oh, I know he went on about damaging this place's reputation and all that sort of thing, but there could be another reason, couldn't there?' She smiled brilliantly and turned her slim bare shoulders round to Kyle. 'Do me up, darling,' she instructed. 'I don't want to be late downstairs. Oh, and don't forget—Fier says you're to do the coffee tonight, not me. That was probably what he was so cross about.'

With her knack of seeing things only as she wanted them to be, Grace had already rationalised the scene with Fier. He was jealous—and he was annoyed with Kyle! And who was she to say that Grace's version was incorrect? Kyle ran the zipper smoothly up Grace's back. Fier had certainly criticised her that morning for leaving Grace behind the coffee tray, and as for being jealous?—although that didn't fit the personality she knew, Grace's effect was almost always revolutionary.

She was so beautiful in the unmistakable Oscar de la Renta dress: Fier certainly wouldn't be the first man to have had all his ideas changed.

'There you are!' Zip fastened and tiny hook secured, she stepped back.

'Thank you, darling.' Grace turned and gave her a dazzling smile. 'How do I manage to get along without you?'

Very well indeed, it seemed, Kyle thought wryly as she followed the bare neck and shoulders to Grace's bedroom door and closed it behind them after switching out the light. But what was she so envious about? She also had improved.

She hadn't seen Fier since he had left her office on the ironic, semi-mocking comment, but she would that evening and that, doubtless, would be when the rest of Grace's theory would be proved totally correct.

Walking along the landing and down the stairs, she became conscious that the folds of her much simpler lace and cotton insert dress were clinging to her legs. The air was dry up here, full of electricity, and although she wore a petticoat, she had forgotten to spray it with anti-static spray so that her skirt clung in far too intimate a way to what Grace called her 'showgirl' legs. She twitched it free. Not that she had to worry. With Grace ahead of her, blonde hair shining and graceful neck and shoulders satiny-white above the striking contrast of midnight blue shot silk, who was even going to notice who was in her wake?

Grace had made her later than she usually was and

there were two people already in the lounge when they got down. Two heads turned in their direction. One immediately turned away but the other stayed watching them with hard, unblinking eyes. The LaRocques! It had been the husband who had looked away, as apparently intent on a large painting above the stone fireplace as if he was seeing it for the first time and Madame LaRocque who had stayed watching them.

'Good evening, Countess—Miss Haultain.' She acknowledged Kyle almost as an afterthought, moving towards them with the practised smile of the wife behind a successful politician; only the eyes remained unchanged. 'What a delightful gown, Countess. One of the benefits of travel, I suspect—so much more choice of where to buy your clothes!'

It was easily and naturally done. Manoeuvring Grace to one side, talking first and then drifting towards the chesterfield until they were sitting down with her own spare, upright figure between Grace and the man still studying the picture with his back to them.

Fier, it seemed, had not been the only one to have a few sharp words to say about Grace's effect on Guy LaRocque the night before.

'Miss Haultain, could you come into the dining room for a moment?' Charlene, suddenly appearing at her elbow, demure in black and white, was clearly panicking.

'Of course.' Briefly aware of Fier walking towards Guy LaRocque and of Ben in the background with his tray of drinks, Kyle followed her. Monique LaRocque hardly had to worry. Although flirting came as naturally to her as breathing, Grace wasn't going to bother with Guy LaRocque tonight.

'I don't know how it happened!' Charlene was too

emphatic. 'I wasn't even near it when it went!'

Inside the dining room, the floral centrepiece on the table had somehow managed to tip over. There was water everywhere and bruised and broken flowers. 'Well, don't just stand there!' Kyle snapped her exasperation. 'Go and get a cloth!'

It was an inauspicious start to an inauspicious evening. The flowers were easily dealt with and a new centrepiece of fruit produced to take their place, but the obvious tension between the LaRocques communicated itself to the other guests.

'You will forgive me, won't you?' It was still early when Grace started making her excuses soon after the LaRocques had gone upstairs. The Smythes had followed them, so only the Samuels were hovering when Grace stood up to say goodnight. She smiled charmingly at the couple. 'Please don't let me break up the evening, but I really am so tired!'

Of course they would forgive her. Anybody would. Kyle would have forgiven her herself if she hadn't spent her life with Grace and Thea and known what splendid actresses they both, in their own way, were.

And tonight Grace had been giving a tremendous performance. Not enough of a change to make it obvious; just enough to make the previous night's attention-seeking glitter seem like nervousness or else over-tiredness caused by her long journey. Monique LaRocque had obviously been having second thoughts, and as for Fier, if regret hadn't been so foreign to his nature, he, too, would have probably been regretting his earlier tongue lashing.

His eyes had rarely left her; following her everywhere with the inner glint of their own quiet private smile, and now he was openly smiling down at her as

Grace stood on tiptoe to kiss the cheek of the man who, she had earlier been earnestly explaining to Hettie Samuels, was not only a distant cousin but 'the only man I have left to turn to in the world!'

Poor Alex! Kyle suddenly thought of him. Poor Kyle! Poor Fier! No—not poor Fier. Judging from the expression on his face as the soft and scented body brushed against him and the pink lips touched lightly on his cheek, he was half in love already.

'Goodnight, Kylie!' Now it was her turn to be kissed. Her turn to be enveloped in the fragrant aura and feel the brush of those soft pink lips against her cheek. How could Fier not fall under the spell of that enchantment? And how could she possibly hate the girl who was her sister?

'Goodnight, everyone!' With a final smile, Grace's slender back and shoulders disappeared around the carved banister at the top of the flight of stairs, and after a few platitudes, the Samuels followed her.

At last! Kyle stood up from her place behind the coffee tray and moved her shoulders in a little stretch. At last she was released from her duties as Fier's hostess and the strain of hiding everything underneath a smile. 'Goodnight,' she said it generally to the two people left in the room.

'Just a moment—I want to talk to you.'

An evening that had seemed to be dragging on for ever was still not going to be allowed to end. With Ben quietly gathering glasses and emptying ashtrays in the background, Fier interposed himself between Kyle and the longed-for escape route of the stairs.

'Can't it wait until tomorrow?' She deliberately kept her eyes focussed on the few wisps of Tio Pepe-coloured hair falling across her forehead so that the shape behind them stayed an indeterminate blur.

'If it could have waited, I wouldn't have asked you to stop now,' Fier said pointedly. 'Besides, it's early yet.'

Was it? She started to look past him towards the clock, but her eyes betrayed her and brought him into startling clarity. He was wearing a white dinner jacket tonight. White jacket, white shirt, black tie and trousers; dark skin with the faint grain of his beard on his lean, incisive jaw and the slight twist of his mouth the only curve in a face of otherwise hard straight lines and planes.

Aware of the jolt of physical recognition spiralling through her, Kyle forced her eyes to move on past and bring the hands of the little carriage clock on the mantelpiece into focus. Did they really say only just ten past ten o'clock? Had an evening that had seemed never-ending really only started a bare three hours before?

'Are you satisfied?' Her answer came from the wry voice on a level with her forehead and she looked straight up into eyes that were frankly dancing above a mouth that was appreciably more curved. 'Is it really such an imposition to stop and talk to me?' His amusement made her feel acutely uncomfortable.

'What do you want to talk about?' she said, and flushed.

He turned, lamplight catching the sheen of dark hair above broad shoulders. 'That'll do, Ben,' he ordered quietly.

'What?' The white-coated barman glanced across from his tray half filled with glasses and another pair of eyes went back and forth between them; knowing. 'Oh, yes, Mr Cailloux—sure!' Man, tray and glasses disappeared through the far door and then there was nothing except the two of them and the lamplit room.

'Why don't we sit down?' Fier nodded towards the couch.

'No—no, thank you, I'd rather stand.'

'As you wish.' He stood over her, weight lightly balanced, hands thrust in trouser pockets and thighs arched, but the dancing flecks in the cobalt eyes had disappeared and so had the smile. And that was how she wanted it; formal, at arm's length, no matter what Ben thought. 'Were you planning on going into Edmonton tomorrow?' She had nothing to complain of in his tone of voice. The only warmth in the room came from the shaded lamps.

'Yes.' She could be just as curt.

'Then I'd like you to postpone.'

'Really? Why?' A flicker of interest broke through her façade; he had never monitored her trips before.

'Because I want you to take Grace with you when you go.'

'But she can come with me tomorrow.' There was no reason why she shouldn't. It was a routine weekly trip. No guests to take in or bring back from the airport; no extra load. If Grace wanted to do some shopping she could leave her downtown at the Bay and pick her up when she had finished with her business. Taking Grace to the warehouse and putting her in range of the importer's roving eye would be just asking for trouble; Kyle was still having her problems with the man.

'She can't,' Fier answered shortly, 'she'll be with me.'

'Of course!' Kyle looked away. She'd been a fool not to have guessed. Of course Fier would want Grace with him for the first few days. She wondered if he knew she couldn't ride—but that was probably part of the attraction. The Chicken King's wife had certainly enjoyed the body contact of being lifted up into the saddle and having Fier's fingers place hers on the reins; now it was Fier's turn. 'Then I'll go alone tomorrow,' said Kyle in the general direction of the room at large.

'I'm afraid the helicopter won't be available.'

'But——' It took a moment for it to register. Six guests, Fier and Grace; there was room enough for all of them in one of the two big Bell 206's. So there had been a change of plans—Kyle tried to tell herself not to let it hurt so much. So Fier and Grace were flying off to picnic and take pictures and not going on a ride. The planning of the daily activities at Faucon d'Or had nothing to do with her. There would be no need to tell her of any change of plan. Only Mace and the wranglers need be told that the horses wouldn't be required, and they would probably be pleased with the extra time off anyway. 'Oh!' A lead lump came along with understanding and settled in her chest. 'I see.'

'Do you?' His sarcastic drawl wrapped round her. 'Or are your eyes as usual tightly closed when it comes to seeing anything about Grace?'

Kyle bit her lip. He might be gibing and sarcastic but—oh, how wrong he was! She saw everything when it came to Grace; he was the one, like every other man, who either didn't, or didn't choose to see the thought processes going on behind that lovely face. Although the evidence had been totally against her, she had still found herself hoping against hope that he had seen through Grace's act that night, but he had obviously been as taken in as everyone else had been.

'I assume you mean that you're taking one of the

helicopters with Grace and that the guests are going in the other one with Mike and, presumably, with Mace.' She tilted her chin and faced him, determined not to let him guess.

'Yes—presumably with Mace.' He said it quietly, standing over her, his irritation of a moment earlier replaced by a slightly meditative look which gave his eyes a sheen and caught her twin reflections in them, head tilted back, chin stubborn and sherry eyes under a soft crown of sherry-tinted hair quite brilliant and dry.

Please don't look at me like that, she begged silently. 'In that case, I'll take her with me Friday,' she said stiffly.

'I'd prefer it if you went next week.' The look had gone. 'I'll let you know which day.'

Kyle shrugged with an effort at indifference. 'It doesn't matter.' Why shouldn't she fly into Edmonton next week—and not bother to come back? Grace could give some sort of explanation if, that was, Fier even bothered to ask for one. 'And now if you'll excuse me. . . .' She turned defeatedly away.

'It doesn't take much, does it?' She had three steps to go towards the stairs, but he stopped her before she had taken the first one. Oh, no, not more! She didn't think she could bear any more. She stood there, arms hanging by her side, fists clenched, hearing him come up behind her.

'Doesn't take much to do what?' At least she still had her back to him. At least he couldn't see her face. All she had to do was keep her voice under some sort of control.

'To drive all the spirit out of you.' She could feel him watching her.

'I'm sorry,' she said huskily. 'I'm just tired, that's all.'

'Dammit, Kyle!' Hands bit into her shoulders and swung her round. 'Will you please stop being sorry! Why must you be like this?'

Outshone by Grace and Thea; totally forgotten by her father in the last years of her life. Was that what he meant? But she didn't ask and Fier wasn't listening. Instead his fingers held her with the fierceness of frustration and the face bent over hers was dark and angry.

'What does it take to get you to understand?' he demanded passionately. 'What does it take to get you to *hear* what I want to say?'

Of course he was frustrated, Kyle's thoughts ran on. She could feel the urgency, see the need. It should have been Grace he was holding at arm's length, not her. Another thought formed in her head—awful, frightening.

If she took a step towards him, her body, already swaying of its own volition, would be hard against him. And would that matter? Would it really matter if once, just once, she allowed herself to know what it was really like to be possessed and held and loved? With closed eyes, would he really know that it was her he was making love to and not Grace?

'Can't you make room for anything in your skull except your own opinion of yourself?'

His angry voice came from a long way off, lost in the blood pounding in her ears. She had never known she could feel like this. Empty, light, longing to be kissed—and more than kissed.

She watched the movement of the thin dark mouth, lost to the meaning of the words as she remembered how it had felt moving against hers and how the hands now tightening on her shoulders had once before held her equally furiously when he had flung her on her bed and accused her of encouraging the long since departed Canadian billionaire. She had also felt them quietly beside a mountain stream, but Fier had taught her how to feel a stronger passion and that was what she wanted now. And she didn't only want to take— but give.

She longed to arch herself against the smooth dark satin of his flesh and feel him trembling, as she was trembling now, and she longed to take him with her into passion.

But what would happen then? An ice-cold chip of sanity started to return. She could run her hands across his eyelids, feather-light, but the moment had to come when those eyes would open and he would see that it was Kyle he was holding to him—Kyle, not Grace.

'No!' His mouth was still moving, but it was her voice that she heard. 'Please—let me go!'

She couldn't stop, couldn't stand there waiting for the understanding to dawn in those turbulently angry eyes. She didn't want his pity, and what could he have for her but pity if he realised that she had been dreaming she could ever be a substitute for Grace?

She gathered her clinging skirt around her legs and fled from him up the stairs, ignoring the pain from his fingers on her shoulders and deaf to the authority in the voice that followed her.

She was Kyle Haultain; not Grace or Thea. She was the one everyone overlooked. Ash had been the first man to teach her that. The reality was more than twenty years ago, but she could still remember as if it had been yesterday the look on her father's face as he had hung over a net-draped cradle and the five-year-old girl standing next to him, loving him so much, had ceased to exist.

And, like Ash Haultain, Fier was obsessed by Grace. That was why he had brought *her* here. Not to fill the gap caused by his dismissal of Marsha Vincey; not because she, personally, meant anything to him, but because where she went, sooner or later, Grace was bound to follow.

The thought that had lurked uneasily beneath the surface of her mind for weeks took on sickening form and shape as she leaned shivering against the refuge of her bedroom door. Grace was destitute—or would have been—Grace was also without a home; of course she would be bound to come to Faucon d'Or, particularly if the one person she had turned to all her life was already there.

God, what a fool she was! Kyle felt nauseous and defeated. She should have realised when Fier had asked her about Alex—making sure the way was clear—and before that, when he had told her not to send Grace any money. He had been gradually narrowing Grace's options just as she herself had been left without a choice when he had summoned her to his mountain hideaway. She had never quite accepted his explanation. She had had a choice—that was true enough—but when everything had been arranged for her—her ticket, her papers, her work at Dovercourt handed over to Ted Sully—what real alternative did she have except to come to Canada? As bait!

'Goodbye, darling! Don't work too hard!'

Kyle hadn't meant to be anywhere near the helipad the following morning when Grace and Fier left for their day alone, but of course, she was. Drawn by an irresistible urge for self-punishment, she told herself cynically.

'Goodbye.' She inclined her cheek for Grace's kiss, trying to ignore the look of triumph. As Grace had so rightly pointed out, she hadn't made any progress with Fier and she had been alone with him for months. Why then should Grace feel any guilt? 'Have a good day.'

'I will!' Grace was positive. 'But my, you're cold! You're shivering!' She laid her hand against Kyle's cheek.

'No, she wasn't cold. She just didn't seem to be able to stop shaking. But at least it wasn't visible. Only someone touching her would know.

'Why don't you go inside?' Grace suggested. 'There's no need to wait and see us off!'

No, there wasn't. There was absolutely no need to inflict more pain and watch as Grace, in figure-hugging pants and white bomber jacket with a glimpse of brilliant aquamarine from the scarf around her neck, walked arm in arm with Fier across to the waiting helicopter and the beginning of their first real opportunity to get to know each other.

'Darling, you're not sick, are you?' Grace not only looked concerned, her concern was genuine. She cared, she really cared; it was only when someone else's interests conflicted with her own that she could be quite ruthless. And Kyle was no longer competition.

'No, I'm not sick—just chilly.' In her short-sleeved dress, Kyle managed a small smile. Another irony; it was going to be a perfect day. Windless, cloudless, the purity of the light making every rock and tree stand out with three-dimensional clarity. Sharp now but with the promise of real heat to come as the sun cleared the mountain tops and shone down on two people lazing on a secluded slope.

'Are you ready?' There was no warmth as Fier came up to them. The eyes might turn the sky behind them into a pale shadow of their blue, but, like the sun, what warmth they held was not to be disclosed until later in the day. They skimmed Kyle now and fastened on to Grace. 'If you are, then we'll get going.'

Night and day! The comparison crossed Kyle's mind as she watched them walk away with Fier's dark head inches above Grace's blonde one. As she had foreseen, Grace had tucked her arm through his and, far from discouraging her, he held it close so that she was forced to adapt her stride to his. Behind them, standing just outside the ranch house door, Guy LaRocque, waiting for the other guests and Mace, was also watching them. He, too, must be admiring them—might also be comparing them to night and day, but what he couldn't know was that the night Kyle had in mind was the one from which she thought she had awoken but had now clamped down again.

Why had she had to come so far? Kyle backed away as the rotors on the helicopter began to turn and a pattern of swirling dust made its way towards her. If only she had known, she could have fallen in love before. The young solicitor at Dovercourt—what was his name?—she could have married him, but she hadn't realised, and he had lost interest and gone away. Unlike the Sleeping Beauty, it hadn't taken just a kiss to wake her up—it had taken the complete upheaval of her life. It had taken Fier. And she had had to come four thousand miles to discover what he meant to her—and lose him.

The helicopter lifted off and banked, apparently almost falling from the sky as it veered clumsily towards the north. Behind her, the other guests had begun to gather, some watching the now steady flight, others intent on the preparations for their own day as hampers were loaded into the second Bell and Mike, the pilot, straw-haired and easygoing, began to round them up.

What was she waiting for? Kyle shrugged and turned to the small, chattering group with her by now well practised smile.

'Have a good day,' she said as Monique LaRocque went past, and was rewarded with an almost schoolgirl look.

'I'm sure we shall!' The politician's wife's guttural accented voice held satisfaction. She glanced up at the now no more than distant speck of the first helicopter. 'I'm sure,' she said emphatically, 'we shall!'

CHAPTER EIGHT

'ALEX?' Grace had been the first to recognise the figure walking towards the helipad from the open doorway of the ranch house, but even so, her voice was doubtful. 'Alex?' she said uncertainly.

'How are you, Grace?' Now there was no mistaking the stocky outline silhouetted against the setting sun, but even so, Kyle could scarcely believe her eyes.

It had been a long day. Grace talking about Fier; crowing even—and now Alex Orsinski waiting for them when they got back from Edmonton.

'What are you doing here?'

'What do you think?'

The questions and answers went on with Kyle unnoticed. But then when had things been any different? Fier had certainly been glued to Grace's side ever since they had come back from their mountain picnic. She didn't have to guess what had taken place: it was obvious in every word and look as Fier followed Grace with his eyes when he couldn't have her hand in his. She belonged to him—and he to her—the intimacy of lovers needed no interpretation, and Kyle had deliberately buried her head underneath her pillow every night, not knowing and not wanting to have the confirmation of voices coming through the doorway of her room. It was enough to know that she had been the last to leave the lounge—except for Fier and Grace. Perhaps they whispered, perhaps they didn't talk as Fier went to Grace's room, or she to his, but whichever bed they chose, she didn't want to know.

She only had the expression on Grace's face each morning and Grace's never-ending conversation on their way to and back from Edmonton.

Grace! There had been other women in Fier's life. There must have been. A man in his late thirties . . . of course there must have been. He had even told her about one: the girl in Paris who wouldn't come to Faucon d'Or and who was now married with two children. He had drawn her to him after he had told her that, and she remembered the experience of the hands, the mouth, the body touching hers—but Grace! It was as if he had been waiting all these years—and Grace had been waiting, too. With Fier, the mastery would be absolute. There would be no flirtations, no easy letting go. Faucon d'Or might now be sacrificed, but Grace had met her match.

She was a coward; Kyle acknowledged that. She should have come straight out and asked Grace. But hearing it—knowing she was right—made hoping against hope impossible.

'Hey, you forgot the mail!' Mike's voice coming from the open doorway of the helicopter made Alex turn towards her. Of course—there was *another* Haultain sister! Holding the bundle of envelopes Mike tossed in her direction, thinner than usual and packaged by someone in the post office in Edmonton, Kyle walked towards him.

'Hallo, Alex.' Was her smile as forced as it felt? She hoped not. She liked Alex; wished him luck with Grace, but what had luck got to do with it? Alex's loss was just as predestined as her own had been since the moment Grace Haultain had been born and a boy then in his teens, part-Cree, part-Iroquois, part-French and only one part Haultain, had been growing up in the mountains now encircling them.

'Kyle—it's good to see you!' The warmth and the smile were also genuine. 'I got the shock of my life when Cailloux told me you were here! Nearly dropped the telephone!'

Fier had told him? Kyle didn't understand. But her shock that Fier had obviously taken the trouble to patch through a call on the ranch's radio to Alex's villa on the edge of Cannes was almost smothered in a hug that could have come straight out of a film by Eisenstein.

But Alex's hug was the only Russian thing about him—other than his name. The Orsinskis had been away from Russia for too long and there had already been more French than Russian blood even before they had been forced out by the Revolution. And Alex's father had followed the example that his ancestors had set by marrying a girl he met in the French underground resistance during the war. The result was that Alex was pure French in upbringing and manner. It was only the blond hair and slightly Slavic eyes that hinted at his deeper ethnic background; those and, of course, the tremendous bearlike hug from which Kyle now extricated herself.

'Alex!' It was good to look up into a man's face in such an uncomplicated way, smiling and seeing him smile back at her with nothing hidden behind the eyes. 'What are you doing here?'

'I've come to take Grace home.' It was a ukase worthy of a Russian Czar. Alex had changed in his approach to Grace, Kyle thought fleetingly.

'And I'm not going, and you can't make me!' For once left on the outskirts of a conversation, Grace broke in sulkily. And yet, behind the petulant droop of the pink lips and the stubborn expression on the face, there was a glint—a gleam. Alex had come five thousand miles to get her. It was flattering. It wasn't likely to give him an edge over Fier, but Kyle sensed Grace was seeing an Alex she had never seen before.

'I'm not going to drug you or tie you up.' Alex's agreement was amiable enough. 'But you'll come—you have my word on that!'

He *was* different. The kid gloves were off. Behind the outward amiability, a core of sheer hard purpose had replaced the earlier infatuation that had had him treating Grace like a fragile piece of china—or a child whose every whim had had to be indulged.

But—poor Alex, he was too late. Another man had stamped his mark on Grace and he was harder, stronger, even more determined. Doubtless that was why Alex had been summoned to Faucon d'Or: so that Fier could prove, once and for all, that there was no point in entering a battle Alex had already lost. He might just as well agree to a divorce and let Grace go.

But there was no sign of letting go as Alex took Grace by the elbow and turned her in the direction of the path leading down into the valley. 'How are your shoes?' He glanced at the flat metallic pumps at the end of bone-coloured pantyhose. 'Good!' He was satisfied. 'They'll do.'

'Why?' Grace scowled at him suspiciously.

Alex pressed her arm more securely to his side and smiled. 'Because I don't want you to be uncomfortable—and we're going for a walk.'

'Kyle!' Grace wanted rescuing, but Kyle refused to interfere. At least let Alex have his chance. Later would be time enough to discover that he had no hope. Later, when he saw Grace with Fier.

The two fair heads had already disappeared beneath the level of the plateau by the time Kyle had walked away from the helipad and up the short path to the house. Behind her, Mike and two or three of the wranglers were talking as they pushed the helicopter into the open-sided hangar in which it lived with its blue and white-painted twin. Fier, she supposed, had flown into Edmonton in the second chopper and brought Alex from the airport while she and Grace had been downtown.

It was strange. After one or two postponements, it had been Fier who had decided they should at last fly into Edmonton that morning, and it would have been sensible, and much more economical, to let Alex come back with them. However, having taken the trouble to contact him and persuade him all the way from Cannes, she supposed it was only logical that Fier would want the opportunity of a few words alone with the man standing between his future wife and freedom.

It was strange, though, how Alex had taken it. The old Alex would have been belligerent or extravagantly depressed. The new Alex just seemed determined to get Grace back.

So—Kyle gave up the puzzle—Fier had been in Edmonton and she hadn't known. Yet another example of the many things that went on at Faucon d'Or about which she was totally unaware. It wasn't that she closed her eyes; just that most of the time her own part in bringing five-star comfort to the wilderness kept her so preoccupied that she had neither the time nor inclination to concern herself with anything for which she was not immediately responsible—the comings and goings of the helicopters, the operation of the radio room or any of the other thousand and one aspects of the ranch that Fier supervised himself.

It was only recently—since Grace had arrived—that she had deliberately shut her eyes.

Fier had been right in that. She didn't want to know, didn't want to see or hear what she couldn't change. Avoidance had become the hallmark of her behaviour; maybe that was why Fier had left her to find out for herself that, when the Samuels and the Smythes had flown out with her and Grace that morning, there would be no one flying back to take their place.

The LaRocques had left the day before, their departure a relief all round underneath the practised smiles, so now there were just the four of them. Herself, Alex, Grace and Fier; all related by blood or marriage and all tied, one way or another, by the painful bonds of love.

She reached the sprawling, log-built house and crossed the dividing line between the perfect peace and gold of a mountain summer evening and the comparative chill and shadow of the hall.

'Where's Grace?' The voice that came from even deeper shadow startled her.

'She's still outside.' Kyle wondered why she had bothered to be startled. Of course Fier would be waiting. He had hardly left Grace's side for the past five days. The nights were something at which she could only guess, but, whenever Grace appeared, Fier was at her side—attentive, all-absorbing: no wonder Grace had had eyes for no one else. 'Alex met us from the chopper. They've gone for a walk.'

She could also be abrupt. She could also hurt. After a day spent listening to Grace's plans, she at least deserved that much.

'He'll sell the ranch, of course.' After a rare few minutes' silence on the flight back, Grace had turned to her with absolute certainty and a fist had hit Kyle squarely in the stomach.

Sell Faucon d'Or? She remembered the French girl with whom he had been in love and, most of all, she remembered the intensity in Fier's voice. His grandfather had run for seven days and seven nights to get the land on which the ranch now sat. And yet was it really so incredible? Grace had that effect on men. And after Faucon d'Or, would it be Dovercourt's turn to be sold? 'I see,' she had said tonelessly. 'Have you decided when?'

Instead of answering, Grace had narrowed her incredible violet eyes. 'Oh, Kylie, I'm so sorry! You're still stuck on him, aren't you? I'm sorry—I really am!' What had happened to everything being fair in love and war, Kyle had wondered fleetingly, and what had happened to Grace's original suggestion that she should marry him?—but it was genuine. The sympathy in the perfect heart-shaped face, the warmth in the hand that had come out to cover hers, it had all been genuine.

Just as Fier's infatuation for Grace was genuine. It must be—had to be—if he was prepared to sacrifice his wilderness. That was why she knew her ears were now deceiving her.

'Good.' The single word reached her from the shadows of the hall inside the ranch and, as her eyes adjusted from the light outside, she could see him smile. 'Good,' he said again.

'But I said Grace had gone for a walk with Alex!' An inner force for self-destruction drove her to enunciate every syllable.

He began to walk towards her. 'And I said good!' His eyes were shining in the semi-darkness, his mouth was quirked and his whole face was vibrant and alive. 'That gives us a chance to talk.'

'What have we got to talk about?' She couldn't let him touch her. Not that he was making any attempt to do it physically, but the way he stood there, head inclined, eyes ranging over her, sent a shiver of memory running down her spine. 'Faucon d'Or?' She heard herself over-compensate with the stiffness in her voice, but she couldn't—daren't—let him guess. 'Or is it Dovercourt you want to talk about?'

'Dovercourt—Faucon d'Or? What have they got to do with it—especially Dovercourt? One day, there'll be sons enough to inherit both of them.'

Of course there would be! Kyle didn't miss the passionate conviction in his voice. His and Grace's sons. Fier Cailloux wouldn't only sire two daughters. And once she might also have believed him. His rare flash of bewilderment when she had mentioned the estates had been good enough to be genuine—but genuine was a word she had learned to mistrust.

'I heard you were selling them,' she said off-handedly.

'Selling them?' His brows met in a straight black line.

'Grace. . . .'

He let her get no further. His head went back and chin and throat were briefly arched above her. 'And you believed her?'

'Why shouldn't I?' she asked stiffly.

'Yes, why shouldn't you?' He was suddenly and completely serious. 'I should have learned by now that you suspend all powers of judgment where your family is concerned!'

'What is there to judge?' she enquired icily. 'It's obvious.'

'What's obvious, Kyle?' He challenged her with his intensity. 'That your father was a weak man whom you've allowed to cripple you emotionally and spiritually all your life? Isn't it about time you stopped blaming yourself for being a little bit too bright and a little bit too competent to fit into Ash Haultain's image of the perfect daughter and learned to like yourself?'

'You have no right . . .!' she began, but he wasn't listening.

'Or is it Thea?' he demanded angrily. 'Judge her if you like—having another man's child and claiming it as your father's. Oh, don't be surprised,' he sneered cuttingly. 'She told my mother. She told me. In some families, we're not frightened to communicate!'

'Then Grace isn't . . .?'

'Ash's child?' He supplied it for her. Something she had always known, perhaps, but never wanted to accept. Thea's hair, her face, everything about Grace came from their mother. No wonder Ash had been in love with her. He had been unable to hold the mother, so he had transferred all his need for affection to the child. No wonder Grace had run away to her disastrous first marriage. 'I see you understand!' Fier read her face. 'But maybe what you don't appreciate is what's happening now.'

Oh, yes, she knew that well enough, and Fier's disclosure had made it even clearer. There were no ties of blood to bar them; Fier could have his sons. Unlike her, he and Grace were not related—however distantly.

'I invited Alex here——'

'To tell him it was useless!' this time she cut in.
'You say that I can judge my mother, but I can understand what she did!' She of all people could understand. She had also suffered through Ash's indifference. His way of blotting out everything and everyone
he didn't want to know. It had been defeat, maybe, a
symbol of his weakness, but was it really so surprising
that he had driven Thea to look for love elsewhere? In
a curious way, she had never felt closer to her mother
than she did now when they were four thousand miles
apart.

'To tell Alex what was useless?' Fier picked up her
earlier thought. 'That pampering Grace—begging for
her affection like a replica of Ash Haultain—was the
surest way of driving her away. Don't you think Grace
was frightened—or are you so bound up in feeling
sorry for yourself that you're quite incapable of realising what other people feel?' His voice was raw and
jagged. 'You're self-centred and quite stupid. I'm an idiot
to have fallen in love with you!'

Shock hit her with the impact of an earthquake. He
was lying; she knew he was. Covering up, trying to
hide what he guessed she had discovered. 'In that case,
you needn't worry.' She saw his eyebrows rise. 'I re-
lease you. You're quite free. Ask me nicely and I might
even be a bridesmaid at your wedding!'

She didn't know she had such anger in her. All she
knew was that he had made it impossible for Grace not
to follow her to Faucon d'Or, and now he was pretending it had been for Alex's sake.

She watched the skin tighten on his face. 'And what
exactly does that particular comment mean?' he gritted
out.

'Exactly what it says! I wish you joy with Grace.

And now, if you'll excuse me, I have some work to do!'

He caught her wrist as she started to go past him. 'Not before I've finished what I've got to say!'

'You mean there's more?' Kyle tried for sarcasm and found it and the manacle of his fingers loosened on her wrist. 'What can it be, I wonder? You've already told me Grace isn't Ash's daughter and that Thea's an adulteress! What other skeletons have you unearthed from the Haultain family cupboard?'

'Damn you, Kyle!' She heard the rumble of his growl as she went blindly on.

'Oh, yes,' she managed a brittle little laugh, 'there was one more thing, wasn't there?' Her tongue just wouldn't stop—lashing out, hurting as she had been hurt so many times before. 'I'm self-centred and quite stupid, but you're in love with me!' Now she stopped and looked at him directly in the eye, her own eyes brilliant and quite hard. 'And now I think it's my turn to tell you something,' she said bluntly. 'I don't believe a word you say!'

Fier looked at her for a long, long moment. 'No,' he said, 'I didn't think you would.'

He was halfway up the stairs before she thought to stop him—how dared he play cat and mouse with her?—but a shadow moved within the deeper shadow of the stairwell and blocked her way.

'Let him go!' Mace's affinity to Fier had never been more obvious as he stood there watching her with aged yet ageless eyes. 'Don't drive him away!'

'Drive him away?' Kyle was incredulous. 'We couldn't be farther apart than we are now!'

A door slammed above them. A man was making his way across his eyrie of a den to stand beside the picture window, arms crossed, brooding, gazing blindly out at the distant peaks.

Mace had heard it, too. 'Then don't make it impossible for yourself to stay on here,' he said implacably.

It was a long time before her breath started to come normally. For the first time in her life she had let rip with her emotions and, in doing so, she had lost what she wanted most. But of course Fier didn't love her—it had been words, just words. And Mace was wrong. They would never be reconciled.

The tiny clasp on the necklace she had planned to wear that evening failed to respond to angry fingers and she threw the whole thing down on to the glass tray on her dressing table.

Of course Fier didn't love her—she hadn't lost a thing!

With no new guests arriving, there were just the four of them that night. Grace, Alex, Fier, herself; an odd quartet around the polished dinner table, full of undercurrents and obliquely misdirected words. Fier in love with Grace and Grace divided—obviously divided—between her latest conquest and the man on whom she had walked out.

There had been a subtle change in Alex: Kyle wondered if she was the only one to see it or the look of puzzlement on Grace's beautiful heart-shaped face as she glanced from Fier to Alex and back again. Something had happened—that was the message in those enormous violet eyes. Fier had not diminished— that would be impossible—but Alex had somehow grown.

There was a touch of Fier about him. The devoted,

almost servile Alex of the past had disappeared. There was a hint of arrogance in the set of the shoulders underneath the immaculately cut white dinner jacket and a hint not just of wealth but of new dominance in the way he treated Grace, and Grace was obviously intrigued.

And how did Fier like that? Kyle wondered. It was impossible to tell from the deeply shadowed face behind the candles and she didn't choose to probe. The possibility that he had been telling her the truth, that he had summoned Alex to Faucon d'Or in an attempt to recapture Grace, was too terrible to contemplate. If that was true, then so was. . . . No! She drew Charlene's attention with a quick shake of her head and a basket of hot dinner rolls appeared in front of her.

'No. No, thank you,' she refused them with an automatic smile. Of course Fier was not in love with her. It was Grace he wanted; Grace he loved. Alex was to be allowed to try again and fail, that was all it was.

It was Fier's misfortune that Alex must have picked up something from him when they had been flying back alone from Edmonton that afternoon which had given him a clue about the best way to treat Grace. He had always been too devoted, too ready to give in; he had just decided to be a little more assertive, that was all.

'. . . What made you decide to do it now?' The conversation going on between the two men began to impinge on her. Alex's voice, relaxed and positive, much less like a rival than a friend. But then Fier hadn't told him yet. He would pick his moment carefully—later, probably, when they could be alone—to tell him that it was hopeless to go on pursuing Grace.

'It's not a sudden decision,' Fier said firmly. 'I've

been thinking about it for some time.'

'And so you're selling Faucon d'Or.' She had missed more of the conversation than she realised, but Kyle didn't miss the note of satisfaction in Grace's voice.

Fier turned to her, eyes lambent in the candlelight. 'No,' he corrected quietly, 'I'm turning it back to what it was always meant to be. A home—a private residence.'

For the two of them, Kyle thought bitterly. So that accounted for the gradual run-down of the guests. And the staff would be the next to go, no doubt, with one Kyle Haultain leading them.

So much for Mace's warning not to make it impossible for herself to stay at Faucon d'Or. Fier had already decided she would be leaving long before he spoke to her. Kyle wondered if Mace had since been let into Fier's confidence. Not that the old Indian wrangler need worry. There would always be a home for him. Master and man; two kindred spirits alone in the wilderness—with Grace.

And yet Grace had been so convinced that when he married her, Fier would be selling Faucon d'Or. Either Grace had failed for once or Fier had broken a promise—but it was too much to try and work out now. She was tired, confused, and a lump of lead had settled round her heart.

'Excuse me.' The scrape of her chair against the hardwood floor reminded three people of her existence.

'Kyle!' Fier called after her, but she ignored the autocracy in the hard, clipped voice. There were no guests seated at the long table, just the owner of that voice and Grace and Alex. She was no longer duty bound to stay and smile and carry on polite conversations for appearances' sake, regardless of the anguish that stabbed through her every time she happened to glance up and catch Fier watching her. Tonight she could be herself, and that self said leave—now, at once, before she gave herself away.

Leave the field to Grace and the two men who were in love with her. Not that the outcome of that particular contest was in any doubt. Alex might have changed his tactics, but it was too late. He had lost to Fier before he had even set foot at Faucon d'Or.

She head no voices coming through her bedroom door that night. There was nothing before she finally fell asleep except one set of footsteps coming slowly up the stairs and pausing at the top. Alex, no doubt. He had realised the inevitable without the need for words and now just Grace and Fier were in the lounge downstairs. Kyle had no doubt that Ben would also have been given an early night. Fier would not require the presence of the barman.

It was Charlene who blocked her way downstairs the following morning. 'I don't know whether to take this up to them or not, ma'am,' she said portentously.

'Take what up to who?' Kyle was not in the mood for games. What was, in fact, a silly question. She could see the loaded breakfast tray in front of her, but the 'who' defeated her.

'The Count and Countess.' Like most Canadians, Charlene enjoyed a title. And Charlene, it appeared, was also enjoying a small intrigue. Her eyes were shining and her usually demure face above the black dress and white apron wore a knowing smile. 'They're neither of them down yet, and the Count's bed's not been slept in!'

Alex had won? It seemed incredible, and yet

Charlene was a usually reliable source of backstairs information. It had been Charlene who had let slip most of the gossip about Marsha Vincey and the scene with Fier that had led to her dismissal; Charlene with her quiet ways and unobtrusive presence who missed very little of what was taking place.

'It's so romantic, isn't it?' Charlene went on happily. 'The Count coming all this way after her and the Countess taking no time at all to fall back in love with him!'

'That's enough!' Kyle spoke abruptly. 'And take that tray back to the kitchen. They'll ring for breakfast if they want it.'

What if it wasn't Alex? That was the question that kept running through Kyle's head. A sure way to dismissal for the staff was getting romantically involved with a guest at Faucon d'Or, but the man who made the rules could break them—and Grace was not a guest. Kyle had already had her suspicions that Grace and Fier were lovers. And even if they hadn't been, what could be more understandable than to choose last night? The final proof for Alex that his case was lost.

Alex's unused bed was another matter. Perhaps Alex couldn't sleep and, if so, who could blame him—perhaps anything. Kyle couldn't—wouldn't—think about any possible explanation. If she went and started work immediately, perhaps she wouldn't think at all.

'Do you have a copy of the staff list?'

There was more than enough time for him to have left Grace sleeping and gone back to his room to shower and shave and put on the familiar blue-grey denims before the door abruptly opened and Fier came into the tiny cubicle of her office.

Everything about him was familiar—too familiar—

and she despised herself for the way her pulses jumped. She had felt those hands, that mouth, that body; she had felt a chord reach out from him to her, but everything she might have hoped for now belonged to Grace.

'Of course!' She refused to look up at him. She produced a typed foolscap list from the top drawer of her desk and handed it to long brown fingers.

Her name was on that paper. Kyle Haultain—housekeeper. If he was turning Faucon d'Or back into a private home, she couldn't—wouldn't—stay.

'Make out cheques for those I've marked and add a three-month bonus.' It seemed an eternity before the list came back to her.

'Of course.' She automatically glanced down. 'But——' Now she looked up, lost, for once, to the familiar shock that spiralled through her as she saw him standing over her, head half inclined and the lock of dark hair falling across his forehead. 'My name isn't marked!' she said incredulously.

'Why should it be?' He was offhanded, curt. 'There's no reason why you should leave.'

How could he be so insensitive? She felt numb. She murmured, 'I think I'd rather.'

'I see.' He watched her coldly. 'In that case——' He took the list. When it came back, her name was marked with a figure written beside it. Her bonus—her reward for being a gallant loser. 'And now, as there seems no point in prolonging a situation which you obviously find distasteful, I suggest you get your things together and fly out with Grace and Alex!'

Kyle knew her ears had been playing tricks long after she had gone up to her room and started packing. Mace and Alex—anyone and Alex; anyone except Grace. And

Fier had given her no chance to ask him to repeat it. She had still been stunned when her office door had closed behind his stiffly rigid figure.

Another door now opened. She had almost finished packing—was at the stage of deciding whether or not to take the black silk dress that seemed to have marked so many stepping stones in her relationship with Fier—when Grace appeared in the doorway of her bedroom. A radiant Grace, glowing in a linen suit with an emerald and diamond ring upon her finger.

She held it out for Kyle's inspection. 'Isn't it fabulous?' she breathed. 'I had to show it to you. You do think I'm doing the right thing, don't you, Kylie?' she added quickly, noticing Kyle's face.

'If you're in love with him, of course you are!' Kyle struggled to put warmth into her voice. It wasn't Grace's fault—not all of it. It took two to make a marriage, after all.

'In love with him? I didn't know I could be so in love! It almost frightens me!' Grace was serious suddenly. 'What if I lose him, Kylie?' she asked anxiously.

'I hardly think you'll do that,' Kyle said drily.

'But he's so different!' Grace insisted. 'I used to think I knew where I stood with him, but I'm not sure now. Oh, I know he gave me this——' she flashed the ring again and it shimmered in the light, like tears, Kyle thought, '—and everything last night was fabulous, but,' she struggled to explain, 'it's like playing a game with someone and winning all the time and then having them change the rules on you!'

Like Fier changing his mind about selling Faucon d'Or, Kyle thought suddenly. 'But you like it here?' she said.

'What?' Grace looked mystified, then her face cleared. 'Oh, yes.' She glanced out of the window at the distant peaks, clear cut and white against a deep blue sky. 'It's lovely! You should have stayed last night, you know,' she remarked conversationally. 'Fier was explaining why he's decided to close the hotel side of it down. He thought that if he brought all the right people here, they would go away and try and save the wilderness, but instead they spoiled it just by being here. You can't have everything, he said.'

No, you can't, Kyle thought bitterly. So Fier was returning Faucon d'Or to the wilderness—the last of the wilderness—with no paths, no noise, no people. Just him and Grace.

'But, Kylie,' Grace had gone back to the subject uppermost on her mind, 'you really do think I'm doing the right thing, don't you? I mean, I couldn't bear it if it all went wrong again, and Alex said that this time, if I walk out, there won't be a second chance.'

The words were difficult to frame. 'Who said there won't be a second chance?' Kyle asked her carefully.

'Alex!' Grace looked surprised. 'Who did you think I meant? Alex has asked me to go back to him, but he says that if I want to go, I've got to change. It's my decision, he said, but if I make it I've got to stick to it. You know, I scarcely knew him,' she shivered at the memory of a few dark moments from the previous night, 'it was like being with someone else! I didn't know he could be so masterful!'

'And so you're going back to Alex?' Kyle said woodenly.

'Kylie, what's wrong with you?' her sister demanded hotly. 'You're not usually this slow! Alex and I are flying out in about half an hour and—Oh, I didn't realise!'

Understanding dawned and she looked quite stricken. 'Oh, Kylie, I'm so sorry!'

'It doesn't matter. . . .'

'But you thought I was talking about Fier!'

'It doesn't matter,' Kyle repeated. 'I'm leaving anyway. I told you, Grace——' she cut across as Grace began again, '—it really doesn't matter!'

No, Grace couldn't speak to him on her behalf. No, she wouldn't change her mind. She was leaving Faucon d'Or today with Grace and Alex. She would go somewhere—anywhere—not to Dovercourt, but there was no need for Grace to worry. She would be all right, and Grace would do best to concentrate on Alex.

Pacified but obviously not convinced, Grace finally left the room, and Kyle continued with her packing. She was like an automaton. Her hands and feet were busy, but her head and heart were numb. What had taken place had happened and there was no way of changing it. She might wish that it could be rolled back and that she could have the time with Fier again, but that was impossible. What was done was done. Alex had warned Grace, but with a man like Fier it was even more impossible that there could be a second chance.

He had told her that he loved her and she had flung his words back in his face.

A knock on the door just as she finished packing announced Mace to get her bags.

'You're leaving, then?'

'Yes.' She turned away from his reproach. Her winter coat was on the bed; she would have to carry it. Mace had also warned her, but she had been too deaf to hear. 'It's just those two cases over there,' she told him.

He picked them up and left and she followed him, pausing on the threshold to look across the room. It was the last time she would see this particular view of the mountains through her window. Range upon range of them, going back into the distance. And, in a few minutes, she would also be having her last look at Faucon d'Or as the helicopter lifted like a wounded bird and veered south towards Edmonton.

Charlene was leaving as well as Grace and Alex and two of the wranglers. Kyle had heard the chattering of the helicopter once before that morning as it had come back from taking another plane-load of staff to Edmonton. When Fier made up his mind, things happened quickly. In a day or two, only he and Mace would be left at Faucon d'Or.

Mace was already taking her cases across by the time she got downstairs and Charlene and the wranglers had already boarded. She could see Charlene peering curiously through the window as Grace and Alex walked across the helipad, Alex possessive but Grace turning and throwing a flirtatious little kiss in Fier's direction. Grace would never wholly change, Kyle thought fondly. Alex might try, but Grace—well, Grace would always be just Grace.

And now there was just one more obstacle to pass. Fier himself, standing in the doorway, clear-cut and unbending with his back towards her. Kyle took a deep breath and walked towards the barrier of bone and muscle she would also never see again.

'Excuse me.' He hadn't heard her. He didn't move and there was no way of getting past him. 'Excuse me!' She tried once more.

In answer, his hand lifted and beyond him, the helicopter blades began to turn.

'Fier!' Her protest was cut off as he swung to face her and she instinctively backed away.

'Come here!' He reached for her and pulled her to him. 'You didn't really think I'd let you go, did you?'

It was after the loving that he turned to her. They were sitting on the chesterfield in his den watching purple shadows stain the mountainside, and it was a new Fier who sat beside her, the pressure of his body close to hers. Tender and warmly gentle, but for her eyes alone. Mace, maybe, had seen this side of him, but few others ever would.

After the loving! Could she ever again doubt that she was loved? Feeling his eyes upon her, Kyle raised her head against his shoulder and looked at him.

The hard line of the jaw above her, the strong throat and, hidden now by the soft fabric of the cashmere sweater, the smooth skin of the muscular body that had at first frightened her but had then aroused her to a sensuous depth of passion she had not known she could possess.

'We're going to have to do something about getting you some clothes!' His hand moved against the sweater covering her bare breast.

'Oh, why?' Content in the satisfied awareness of her body, Kyle answered lazily. She liked the feel of his clothes against her, didn't care that they were too large. Hers had gone off in the helicopter to Edmonton. She supposed, one day, they would come back.

'Because I've no intention of being married to a bride who looks as if she's been dressed by Goodwill Industries!'

Married! She hadn't thought of it! Was she really so unbridled and licentious—she smiled at the oldfashioned nature of the phrase—that she was prepared to be his mistress and not his wife. Her whole body told her that she was as she shifted her weight luxuriously against him and turned to kiss the corner of his mouth.

'Will you please stop doing that?' he commanded gently. 'Have you any idea how many times the thought of you doing that to someone else had driven me quite crazy?'

Yes, once, when he had dragged her away from the doorway of Merle Hubbard's room. She could never forget the Canadian billionaire for that very reason.

She hadn't known that anyone could be so angry, but then she hadn't known the reason. Just as she hadn't known that Fier had deliberately sent for Alex or that Grace's arrival at Faucon d'Or had been as much of a shock to him as it had been to her.

'Grace?' He had turned lazily on his side when she had questioned him, his head beside hers on the pillow. 'Grace is a spoiled child, but she's dangerous. Chasing after LaRocque in front of that dragon wife of his——' his face had tightened at the memory of Grace's open pursuit of the French-Canadian politician. 'I had to do something. Maybe it wasn't original, but keeping her with me all the time was the only thing that I could think of. I couldn't let her destroy everything that Faucon d'Or was meant to stand for. She had influence, that woman and, behind her husband, she had power!'

And Monique LaRocque had flown out, if not convinced, at least pacified. If only she had realised Fier's motive, Kyle had thought ruefully, if only she had not made it impossible for him to explain.

But Fier had been bending his head towards her

breast and, as she had arched towards him, all regret had been lost. It was enough to know that, whatever demands he made of her, she was woman enough to meet them.

The memory of his lovemaking spiralled through her as they now sat on the chesterfield watching the mountains fading into the last of the late summer light.

'Incidentally,' a touch of the old Fier was apparent, 'our first wedding present arrived yesterday!' Kyle looked at him, surprised and he smiled at her confidently. 'You remember Stan Reynolds?'

'Yes.' She remembered the English rock star well enough. How unlike he had been to his public image, just as the man now leaving her and walking towards the built-in stereo was so unlike the man who had mistaken her for the housekeeper when he had arrived at Dovercourt the year before.

'I didn't think slavery was still in fashion!' he had mocked her earlier. 'You infuriated me! Drove me crazy—drove me to do and say things I burned about for weeks afterwards. All I knew was that I had to get you away from those overwhelming womenfolk of yours and see what made you tick, but the closer I got you to me physically, the less you would communicate. You were intelligent and attractive,' he had kissed the end of her nose, 'but not only were you blind to what you were meant to be, you shut your ears and eyes to every attempt I made to tell you. That's why I bought that black dress, I guess. Where is it, by the way?'

The black silk dress with the extravagant dark ruffle on the bodice. Kyle had glanced down at the whiteness of her body lying next to his. 'I suppose it's still in Edmonton,' she had said demurely.

'Listen!' Walking back to his place on the chester-field beside her, Fier commanded her attention.

'Have you heard the sky?' Stan Reynolds' voice came from the stereo. 'Have you listened to what the mountains have to say?'

Fier was next to her and the wilderness of Faucon d'Or stretched beyond the window. Not as it would be—aloof, remote, like the man beside her could be. It still bore traces of the endeavour to which he had given his young years. She, too, had squandered her young years, but they both had the time to come and, in that time, the trails that had been cut for the important visitors would disappear. The wildlife would remain undisturbed and the last of the wilderness would once more take over.

'Have you seen a golden hawk?' Stan Reynolds' voice sent the message to the world. 'Is there space for you to live in—you and me?'

Harlequin® Plus

A WORD ABOUT THE AUTHOR

Sheila Strutt has been a probation officer, hotel receptionist, tobacco puller and journalist. "But nothing," she says, "could possibly equal the totally unforgettable experience of hearing someone talk in a way that shows they've read and enjoyed your work."

Sheila began writing Harlequins while she was living in the province of Ontario, Canada, when for the first time in her adult life she was not going out to work. She and her psychologist husband were building a house, "and someone had to stay back and supervise." So she stayed home and wondered what to do with her free time. Then she happened to see a Harlequin television commercial about love in faraway places.

"I could do that!" she said to herself. And she tried her hand at writing one. Then another.

Her first published Harlequin, *The Master of Craighill* (#2333), was actually her seventh attempt. It appeared in 1980 and was followed by *On the Edge of Love* (#2447) and *Stamp of Possession* (#2496).

Sheila was born in England and trained there as a probation officer. At forty she met and married her psychology lecturer, and today they make their home in Saskatchewan, in the heart of the Canadian prairies.

Winters in Saskatchewan are long and cold, but for Sheila they're the best time of year. The colors are incredibly bright, the sky goes on forever and the sense of space is very special. And, as spring starts to approach in that part of the world, ideas for lovely romantic plots are certain to bloom.

HARLEQUIN
PREMIERE AUTHOR EDITIONS

6 top Harlequin authors — 6 of their best books!

1. **JANET DAILEY** Giant of Mesabi
2. **CHARLOTTE LAMB** Dark Master
3. **ROBERTA LEIGH** Heart of the Lion
4. **ANNE MATHER** Legacy of the Past
5. **ANNE WEALE** Stowaway
6. **VIOLET WINSPEAR** The Burning Sands

**Harlequin is proud to offer these 6 exciting romance novels by
6 of our most popular authors. In brand-new beautifully
designed covers, each Harlequin Premiere Author Edition
is a bestselling love story—a contemporary, compelling and
passionate read to remember!**

Available in September wherever paperback books are sold, *or* through
Harlequin Reader Service. Simply complete and mail the coupon below.

- -

4 FREE Harlequin Romances